RORY

Books by Julia Templeton

SINJIN

VICTOR

RORY

Published by Kensington Publishing Corporation

RORY

JULIA TEMPLETON

𝒜

APHRODISIA
KENSINGTON BOOKS
http://www.kensingtonbooks.com

APHRODISIA BOOKS are published by

Kensington Publishing Corp.
119 West 40th Street
New York, NY 10018

All Kensington Titles, Imprints, and Distributed Lines are available at special quantity discounts for bulk purchases for sales promotions, premiums, fund-raising, and educational or institutional use.

Special book excerpts or customized printings can also be created to fit specific needs. For details, write or phone the office of the Kensington special sales manager: Kensington Publishing Corp., 119 West 40th Street, New York, NY 10018, attn: Special Sales Department, Phone: 1-800-221-2647.

Aphrodisia and the A logo Reg. U.S. Pat. & TM Off.

ISBN-13: 978-0-7582-3817-7
ISBN-10: 0-7582-3817-7

First Kensington Trade Paperback Printing: January 2011

10 9 8 7 6 5 4 3 2 1

Printed in the United States of America

To my readers—
for your loyalty and support over the years.

1

Rory squinted against the early morning light. Dew glistened on the plush, green lawns, and the first glimmer of sun filtered through the tree branches.

All in all, it was a beautiful day to die.

The man at his back started to tremble, and Rory wondered if the quick-tempered lord wasn't regretting calling him out so hastily. No doubt, like Rory, the earl was replaying last night's events in his head and wishing for a different outcome.

The dinner party had been an elegant affair, and from the moment Rory had walked into Lord and Lady Cordland's townhouse, Lady Cordland had set her sights on him. He had no more taken his seat at the dinner table when her hand had clamped on to his thigh. She had then proceeded to give him a come-hither look that could not be misinterpreted.

When she'd left the table between the second and third courses, he followed a discretionary few minutes later, and nearly walked right past her when she reached out and caught him by the arm, jerked him into the parlor, and shoved her hand down his pants.

It had been a fevered and quite exciting coupling, especially given the fact that thirty guests chatted and dined on the other side of the wall, including Lady Cordland's husband and his young mistress, his wife's own cousin.

"We can forget about this with an apology," Cordland said in an unsteady voice, bringing Rory back to the present.

Hell could freeze over before Rory would apologize to the pompous pig. Why was it all right for Cordland to fuck his mistress under his own roof and beneath his wife's nose, but God forbid Lady Cordland do the same?

Rory scanned the park where he had met at least five dozen men in his short life. In the distance, he saw a carriage with the Cordland crest emblazoned on the door, and he wondered if Lady Cordland sat within, awaiting the outcome.

Victor, his brother, had recently mentioned Rory's fondness for fucking only married women. A gross exaggeration, but still, he did prefer married women because they were *usually* so cautious when compared to their younger counterparts. Perhaps he should steer clear of them in the immediate future.

"Do I take your silence as acquiescence?" Lord Cordland asked, his voice hopeful.

"My silence means no," Rory replied matter-of-factly, rolling up his sleeves.

Rory's second, an old friend from Oxford, stood on the sidelines, looking blurry-eyed and terrified that he might have to step in. He need not be so concerned. Rory had never had to use his second.

"Gentlemen, you will walk off ten paces, and when I say turn, you shall turn and fire," the man in charge said in a booming voice that made Rory cringe. His head still hurt from drinking too much whiskey last night, and the pot of tea he had drunk had not helped in the least.

Taking a deep breath, he released it and then lifted the pistol, readying himself for the count.

Damn, but he was still not thinking clearly, and his hand shook, another sign he'd been drinking too much of late. Indeed, it seemed as though he had been in a perpetual state of drunkenness since his brothers had married and he'd realized how ill his father truly was.

Life, which had been fun and exciting for so many years, had suddenly turned lonely, mundane, and exceedingly boring, and the future appeared so bleak . . . especially without his father in it. Their father had always been incredibly kind and patient, save for his latest ultimatum that all his sons marry—an idea no doubt forced upon him by Rory's mother.

Was she really going to push him to marry now that both Sinjin and Victor had done so? In his mind, she was getting greedy. He was the youngest, had the lowest title and the least to offer a bride, so why did it really matter that he marry?

"One, two . . ."

As the count continued, Rory took a step, then another, his mind racing. Life had lost its spark, and he sincerely doubted that finding a wife would help him regain that which he'd lost. Unless she was truly exceptional, but he had yet to find such a woman, even with his mother's assistance.

"Eight . . . nine . . . ten!"

The number was shouted and Rory turned, raised his pistol, and for whatever reason, did *not* pull the trigger.

He heard the roar of his opponent's gun, felt the rip of the bullet tear through his flesh, followed by the sensation of blood seeping through his shirt.

How come he didn't feel any pain?

Lord Cordland's expression was triumphant . . . and then his eyes widened when Rory continued to stay on his feet.

Dizziness washed over him, but he fought it off and cocked the hammer.

The man put his hands out and shook his head. "No, dear God, no!"

Rory frowned. There was a second where he considered sparing the wretched man's life; then without thought of consequence, he squeezed the trigger.

Lord Cordland hit the ground with a gasp, the blow fatal, square between the eyes.

"Bloody good shot!" Rory's second yelled as the surgeon rushed forward, followed by Lord Cordland's second, who glared daggers at him.

Glancing down at the blossoming color on his shirt, Rory closed his eyes as a wave of dizziness came over him.

"My lord," the groom said from directly beside him, his voice tinged with concern.

When had he hit the ground? Rory wondered as the cold, wet grass soaked through his shirt and trousers. He grit his teeth. Oh yes, now he was definitely beginning to feel the pain.

"Get the carriage!" he heard the groom yell. Those were the last words he heard before the world went black.

Shannon was concerned when Lord Graston's younger brother was brought to the Twickenham manor house on the River Thames with a bullet wound to the shoulder.

Thank goodness the surgeon had done his part by removing the bullet and was at the moment stitching the wound closed. There was not much a person could do now but wait to see if fever took hold. She hoped earnestly that her ministrations would help him, because all of London and Rochester would sincerely feel the young baron's loss if he were to die.

Her experience with helping the sick would come in handy

in the days and weeks ahead. While volunteering at the Dublin hospital, death had claimed a good number of the patients, and she had seen and learned enough to realize the young man on the bed was gravely ill. His skin had turned a startling white, almost gray, and the bullet wound was bright red. He had lost so very much blood that she was concerned he would not survive.

Word had already been sent to Lord Graston in Wales, and the rest of the family would be alerted to Rory's condition, but unfortunately, his eldest brother, Sinjin, and his wife were on their honeymoon, and his mother, Lady Rochester, was staying close to her ailing husband at their country estate. The poor woman would be sick with grief and worry when she heard the news about her youngest.

Until his family's arrival, at least the handsome lord would not be lacking in concerned companions. Already all the female servants in the mansion were aflutter, each wanting to tend to the handsome lord; but it had been Edward, Lord and Lady Graston's trusted butler, who had put Shannon in charge of his care. Upon Rory's arrival in a rented carriage, Edward had lined up the servants and asked who had experience in caring for the wounded. She had immediately raised her hand.

Following Edward into the dining room where Rory had first been brought, Shannon had very nearly tripped over her feet when she'd seen the half-naked lord thrashing on the dining room table, where male servants, including her brother, Zachary, did their best to hold him down.

Rory moaned in his sleep, his handsome face wincing in pain as the physician applied the bandage. How she wished Lady and Lord Graston were here. She knew his lordship would go to any lengths to save his beloved brother. Until such a time as her employers returned from their trip to Wales, she would have to do her best to keep him alive.

"Make sure the dressing is changed often," the physician said, putting his items back in his bag. "I shall come tomorrow to check on him."

"Thank you, sir," Edward said, escorting him out of the chamber. He was shutting the door when he paused. "Let me know if you need anything, Shannon."

Shannon nodded. "I will."

Shannon rinsed the rag in the bowl of cool water that sat on a side table beside the bed and looked at her patient. Even pale and wounded, he was beauty personified. A living testament to the male form, like Adonis, so striking he made one pause.

She recalled when last she'd seen him. He'd visited Lady Graston at her London townhouse, and Shannon had served him tea while he awaited Lady Marilyn's arrival. The way he'd watched her through those long, thick lashes had made her nervous. She'd been so dumbstruck by his beauty and attention that it was all she could do to remember her own name.

His hair had been long then, but now it was downright rakish, falling past his broad shoulders and curling up at the ends. His nose was perfectly proportioned, his lips full and lovely, and his teeth white and straight.

With a trembling hand, she wiped his brow with the cool rag, past a chiseled cheekbone, over the strong jaw and chin, to his neck. His pulse fluttered erratically at the base of his throat, and she circled it with her index finger.

Her gaze lingered over his wide chest and flat, muscled belly. She noted a long, silver scar that ran along his ribs, and wondered if, like his current injury, the old wound had been compliments of another woman's husband.

Such a scandalous reputation.

Her cheeks turned pink as her gaze shifted to the sheet that hung low at his hips. Why was it when she was around him she felt hot and sensitive, her nipples tight, and the blood in her veins burned?

As she stared at him, she could not help but wonder what it would feel like to be taken by him, to be one of his many lovers.

Glancing at the sheets bunched about his groin, she once again wet the rag and squeezed out the excess water. Her pulse skittered as her hand moved down the thick cords of his neck, over the wide chest, taking great care to avoid his wound, and swirling around the flat disk of a nipple, before sliding over the muscled planes of his belly.

His cock bucked beneath the sheets. She gasped and swallowed past the tightness of her throat. Before she knew what she was doing, her hand hovered over the sheet, directly above his manhood. Just one peek, that's all. Nothing more.

She glanced at the door, then ever so slightly pulled the sheet down. Her thighs tightened as she stared at the impressive cock: long and thick, and heavily veined with a plum-sized crown. Warmth swirled in her stomach and lower still.

The chamber door creaked open and she jumped, yanking the sheet up with a yelp.

"How is he doing?" Zachary asked, shutting the door firmly behind him.

With heart pumping nearly out of her chest, she released an inward sigh of relief. Thank goodness it was just her brother. Hoping he had not seen what she'd been doing, she licked her dry lips. "It is difficult to say. I just hope he continues to sleep through the night."

"He is fortunate," Zachary said, looking and sounding distracted. "Many would not survive such a wound."

Shannon nodded in agreement and set the rag back into the bowl. "Indeed. I have heard it whispered that he is experienced on the dueling field. The other servants were saying the pistol must have jammed, else the opponent would have never gotten a shot off."

"Or perhaps his luck has run out."

The words held an ominous undertone. She stared at Zachary and could see concern in his eyes.

Fear rushed along her spine. "What is it, Zach?"

He pressed his lips together. His throat convulsed as he swallowed hard. "I'm afraid *our* luck has run out, Shannon."

"What do you mean?" she asked, and she could hear the fear in her voice.

"Clinton has found us."

2

Shannon's heartbeat was a roar in her ears. "Do you mean to tell me you saw Clinton?"

Zachary shook his head. "No, not Clinton. But there was a man that followed me from the livery into the tobacco shop. Whenever I looked over my shoulder, there he was, staring at me."

"Perhaps you looked familiar to him?"

"It is possible," he said in a voice that suggested no such thing. "But every time I glanced at him, he quickly looked away. I have a bad feeling, Shannon. The hair on my neck was standing on end, and I could not shake the feeling of doom I experienced. He has found us. I feel it in my bones."

She hated such talk. For these past six months Zachary had been her rock, the strong one, and she had looked to him to keep her focused and positive. She didn't like hearing him sound so defeated. "What did he look like?"

"I would say fifty years old or so. He had a stocky build, gray hair, and a thick mustache."

"How did you lose him?"

"I darted down an alleyway and passed through the back door of a restaurant."

"He didn't follow you down the alley?"

"I didn't stick around long enough to find out. I was supposed to return to the park to meet Floyd, but I couldn't take the chance in returning just in case the gray-haired man had seen me."

Floyd was Lord and Lady Graston's senior coachman, who had taken Zachary under his wing. The older man often brought him along on errands. "You walked back?"

"Ran is more like it. Floyd picked me up en route. I know he thought I was crazy, especially when I told him that I didn't see him at the park and decided to walk back to the manor. I don't think he believed me. In fact, he kept asking if I was all right."

The last thing they needed was to raise suspicion among their peers. "Well, at least you weren't followed back to the manor."

Zachary raked a hand through his long blond locks. "We need to be on alert. If we see this man again, I'm afraid we might have to start running."

Always it was running. Fear of discovery had been plaguing them since leaving Ireland. Each place they went, they took on one miserable job after another. They rarely spoke of the future anymore, both of them uncertain if they would ever have the freedom they craved.

Working for Lord and Lady Graston had been their best jobs so far, and they both counted the day that Lord Graston walked into Lady Dante's dress shop as one of the luckiest days of their lives.

Because of that fateful encounter, they now had a roof over their heads and three meals a day, plus a generous wage they could not possibly make anywhere else. Lord and Lady Graston had taken them into their household and treated them like family, and the thought of leaving was excruciating.

Some of the fear she was experiencing must have shown on her face because Zachary squeezed her hand. "Do not fret, sister. We just need to be vigilant. Maybe like you said, the man was merely going in the same direction . . . but just to be cautious, I shall request all errands be done by another."

"I think that is wise."

"And you should stay close to the manor as well," he said, walking across the room and looking out the window.

Her stomach twisted into a knot. And here she had started to relax, to not fear and always look over her shoulder. In fact, she had enjoyed her days off where she would go into the city. It had been nice to just get away from the manor. And Shannon had savored those trips, enjoying watching the sights: the finely dressed ladies in their expensive gowns as they walked before pretty storefronts, and handsome men in tailored suits who did more perusing of women than they did the merchandise in the windows.

Those trips served to remind her of the days she and her mother had gone shopping. Her father, though not a titled lord, had made his fortune in business and, in turn, had become a respected member of society. Her family had dined with the wealthiest, most influential people of Ireland, and her parents had hoped she would make a good marriage.

That is, until her parents' untimely death six months ago, when the fire their cousin, Clinton, had started had taken their lives. Her parents had taken in Clinton as a child when his father had been killed in a hunting accident. Her father had given Clinton a home and, as he grew to manhood, a place in his company. Clinton had enjoyed all the luxuries his position had afforded him, but it wasn't enough.

On the night of March 12, under the cover of darkness, he had started the blaze.

Unable to sleep that night, Zachary, smelling smoke and hearing the crackling and popping sounds, looked out the window and saw flames racing up the side of the manor house.

He also saw Clinton walking away from the house and then standing in the shadows of the stables as the manor, where he had been lovingly raised, burned, along with the only family he had.

What no one else knew was that Shannon herself had been awake that night. She'd been unable to sleep after Clinton's discussion with her father. She'd lingered outside the study, surprised at the raised voices she heard on the other side of the door. Clinton had asked her father for a thousand pounds to pay off some bad business dealings. Irritated by his nephew's lack of judgment and rumors of a healthy gambling habit, her father had refused him. Clinton had gone into a tirade and left the house.

She had figured he would blow off steam, but he had done more than that. She heard booted footsteps in the house. Heard the unmistakable sound of wood crackling as the fire worked its way up the stairs, mingling with her mother's screams. Zachary had burst through her chamber door, his eyes wild, confirming what she already knew.

Their parents were dead, and she would never again be the same.

A moan brought her back to the present, and she glanced at her patient. Rory whispered something she could not understand; when he tried to move, he moaned.

"I have made you fret now," Zachary said in a tense voice. "That was not my intention. I just wanted you to know."

"You did the right thing in telling me, Zachary. And you are right. We must do everything we can to stay close to the manor, and pray that he did not follow you here."

"I had better go," Zachary said, already heading for the door. "Don't worry, Shannon. As long as we are together, we'll be all right."

A cold breeze washed over Rory and he flinched.

He had heard voices earlier. Voices with prevalent Irish accents. He'd tried to listen, to follow the conversation, but gave in to the blackness that beckoned.

Every once in a while he heard a calm and soothing voice talking to him, and a gentle hand on his brow, telling him that he would be fine.

Try as he might, he had not been able to open his eyes to that sweet tone and had shortly fallen back into a fitful slumber.

"There, there, beautiful," a woman cooed, and he slowly opened his eyes.

He shifted slightly and winced as a sharp pain tore through his shoulder. His mind scrambled as he tried to focus, and everything slowly came back to him. He had been in a duel with Lord Cordland. The other man had shot him in the shoulder; then Rory had, in turn, killed him.

Only one other time he had been wounded in a duel, and that had been by way of a sword attack when his opponent had struck him across the ribs. The wound had bled like crazy, and had cost him twenty stitches and a scar that constantly reminded him of that stupid liaison he'd had with the head of Parliament's wife. Truth be told, she hadn't been worth the time or effort.

The woman with him now hummed lightly and stared at his cock with obvious interest. He smiled inwardly. If he had to hazard a guess, he had the feeling she was contemplating taking advantage of him.

And he might just let her.

His cock, having a mind of its own, responded, thrusting toward his navel.

"Oh my," she gasped, glancing up at him. "My lord, you are awake."

"Yes, I am awake," he repeated the obvious, and was surprised when his voice came out low and raspy.

A blush rushed up her cheeks, staining them a flattering pink. Close to his age, she had a heart-shaped faced, a bow of a mouth, and amber eyes that were brimming with a desire he recognized only too well. Her curly light brown hair was in a loose bun, tendrils framing her flushed cheeks. "Would you like water, my lord?"

He nodded, his gaze shifting to her large breasts.

She lifted the glass to his lips and watched intently as he took a long drink. Her nipples were erect, straining against the fabric of her uniform. Such lovely, full tits.

"There, there, only a little," she said, setting the glass down on a nearby table. She stuck her ass out and turned to him with a smile. "Can I get you anything else, my lord?"

His lips quirked and his gaze shifted down her body and up again. She had a pleasing figure: a tiny waist, curvaceous hips, and plump bottom. She licked her lips and glanced at his rigid cock once more, before looking toward the closed door. Biting her lower lip, she lifted her skirts high enough to kneel upon the mattress and proceeded to straddle his hips, all without him saying or suggesting a thing.

Taking hold of his cock in one hand, she fisted it, then slid her hand up and down his length. "You're a big one, aren't you?"

His hands moved up her thighs, bringing her skirts up. "Why don't you ride me?" he suggested, wanting to get on with it.

"I really shouldn't," she said, as though trying to convince herself otherwise. Even as she uttered the words, she rose up and slid onto his length with an exquisite sigh that he answered with a deep-throated moan.

She circled her hips, and her inner muscles clamped tight around him. He was too weak to do much, but there was little need since she was doing fine without any effort from him.

He noted the slender wedding band on her left hand and saw the way she kept glancing at the door. Should he be concerned that her husband might walk in, he wondered, the thought vanishing a second later when she leaned down, her tits in his face.

The thin material of her gown provided little barrier to the firm mounds of her breasts, and he sat up slightly and circled the pebbled nipple with his tongue, wetting the gown in the process. She would have to change before returning to her duties. He blew on one peak and then the other, trying to ignore the stabbing pain in his shoulder the slight movement caused.

The exertion may not have been wise. Yet, he could already anticipate the long, blissful nap ahead of him that always came on the heels of sex. Given his current condition, he would no doubt sleep like the dead.

She continued glancing at the door. He had grown to enjoy this game too much, of trying to outwit husbands and lovers.

Lord help his soul, for he might very well burn in hell for all his transgressions.

However, this current transgression was becoming downright boring. His companion was far too concerned about who might walk through the door, to take the lead, and at this rate, it would take an eternity to reach climax.

Mustering as much strength as possible given his injury, he flipped her onto her back and took the dominant position. She gasped and gripped the headboard with both hands, and he slid into her once more. The time for gentle fucking was over. Her breasts bobbed as he rammed into her, his strokes long and steady.

"Ummmm," she said on a moan, meeting him thrust for thrust, her previous preoccupation with the door forgotten as she bit her lip, arched her hips, and cried out as she came.

When the last tremor subsided, she fought to catch her breath, but he wasn't done yet. He went up on his knees and, lifting her legs straight in the air, achieved maximum penetration. Her eyes widened, and he knew she started to climb toward climax again as she licked her lips and focused on his cock sliding in and out of her. He helped her along by playing with her clit, and soon she was urging him on with heated, quite naughty words.

He waited until she came again, and then, never one to be careless, he pulled out of her quivering sex and released his cream onto her belly.

The door creaked opened and the maid beneath him let out a gasp. Rory, hand still on cock, frowned as his gaze caught and held the pretty little maid who worked for his brother and his wife.

Shannon.

Had it been her sweet voice he had heard before?

She stood in the doorway, her hand on the knob, frozen. Her mouth formed an O, and she blinked a couple of times, her gaze shifting between Rory and the maid, and then back again. It wasn't until the maid scrambled off the bed did Shannon slam the door shut. He heard her steps rushing down the hallway a second later.

He looked about the room with its pale silk wallpaper and expensive furnishings. "This is my brother's house," he said, but it really wasn't a question as much as a confirmation. His brother had recently brought his wife the new home on the River Thames.

The maid pushed her skirts down and rushed toward the

door. "Yes, this is your brother's home." She sounded agitated with him, like he had forced her.

"He isn't here?"

"No, he is not, but he has been alerted as to your condition. Your parents, too, my lord."

Oh God. He could already envision his mother's response to the news, running the gamut from shock to fear to anger, but anger would not come until she had seen him with her own eyes.

"I must go, my lord." She stopped for a moment, glanced over her shoulder, her eyes pleading. "I need this job, my lord. I pray that you will not say anything to your brother."

"A gentleman never tells," he replied. Though she might just want to speak to the maid who'd caught them red-handed.

3

Shannon started walking down the hallway, anxious to be as far away from Rory's chamber as she could get. What on earth could Candice be thinking? She was married, for God's sake, and to a handsome footman. Her husband was a good decade older than her, but she herself had told Shannon that she desperately loved Frank.

Shannon had made it to the end of the hallway and had one foot on the stairs when the door to the guest chamber opened.

"Shannon, please wait!"

Shannon stopped and, taking a deep breath, turned to face the other servant. She really wished she hadn't. The material of Candice's bodice was wet, in perfectly formed circles around each nipple, and the taut peaks strained against the uniform.

Candice's gaze followed Shannon's, and when she looked down, her eyes widened. With a horrified groan, she brought her arms to her chest. "Oh my God, what you must think of me."

Shannon lifted her gaze. "You are married, Candice. What could *you* be thinking?"

"I-I could not help myself. He is . . . just so lovely."

That was true, but to throw all caution to the wind and have sex in the same house where one's husband worked? It was wrong in so many ways.

"I asked you to watch him while I had lunch, Candice. I did not think it was too much to ask and that you would—end up doing *that*."

"Please do not say a word to anyone, Shannon. If Frank were to find out, he would kill him."

Or Rory would kill Frank, more like it. Word amongst the staff was that the man Rory had dueled with had been fatally wounded—a perfect shot between the eyes, and that had been after the other man had taken the first shot. If the young baron was such an accurate shot under duress, then Lord help the man who faced him when he was uninjured.

"I will not say a word, I promise," Shannon said, meaning it. She wanted to forget what she had seen in that chamber but knew it would be easier said than done. The image was burned into her mind for all eternity.

"Well, I need to change my gown and return to my duties. Thank you, Shannon. If you should need anything, anything at all, let me know."

Diverting her gaze, Shannon nodded and headed back down the hall, stopping at the linen closet for new bedding. She usually called for her brother to help move Rory, for he was too heavy to move by herself. However, the patient was obviously well enough to move about without assistance. He could just get off the bed while she made it.

Honestly, she should have had Candice do the honors, since she had helped soil the sheets.

Straightening her spine, she tried not to think of Rory and the maid, or the way his hand had stroked his thick manhood as the white substance had pumped onto Candice's stomach.

With a steadying breath, Shannon opened the door to find her patient sitting up in bed, the sheets pulled to his waist. She tried not to focus on his powerful body, but instead set the clean linens on a nearby table. "I would like to change the sheets now. Perhaps you would like me to call for a bath?"

He nodded and slid off the bed, pulled the top sheet with him, and tied it at his waist. Walking toward the window, he stared out. "I did not even realize I was at my brother's home," he said wistfully, his hand moving to his bandaged shoulder.

The room smelled like him—a mixture of musk, sandalwood, and a hint of what Shannon realized must be sex. Once again she tried to forget the image of Rory and Candice with her legs straight up in the air as he made love to her, or the sounds of their mingling sighs as they climaxed together.

As the minutes ticked by, she focused all her energy on her task, anxious to be as far away from the rakehell as possible. She would tell Cook that he was up and needing more nourishment. Perhaps she could send Zachary with Rory's dinner. Let him feed himself.

"It is good to see you again, Shannon," he said, and she glanced up from putting a case on the pillow.

"And you as well, my lord. I hope you are feeling better."

His lips quirked the slightest bit. He had obviously noted the sarcasm in her voice. "The other maid said that my brother has been told of my condition. Have you heard when he will be home?"

"No, but I am sure he will return as soon as possible."

The wicked images of him with Candice fell away. She sensed a sadness about him. She could not help but wonder if that sadness didn't stem from his brother's absence. Family ties had a way of creeping into a person's subconscious when least expected.

21

His teeth brushed along his bottom lip as he turned from the window.

"Are you hungry, my lord? I can ask Cook to make you soup. Does that sound all right?"

He nodded, and she noticed how pale he had become, that there was even a sheen of sweat on his forehead. Her heart gave a jolt as he gripped hold of the window casing. "You must sit," she said, moving toward him, grabbing his arm.

Before she could stop herself, she put a hand to his forehead. "Good gracious, you are so warm."

Taking a deep breath, he then released it. "I do not feel well."

Her pulse leapt at the declaration. Did he have a fever? "Come, you must lie down."

"I would like that bath first, if you do not mind."

"It will take a while to prepare it. In the meantime, as your main caregiver, I must insist you stay off your feet."

His lips curved slightly. "You are my main caregiver?"

She met his gaze directly. "Yes, I have been."

"And how long have I been here?"

"A few days."

"And you have bathed me in that time?"

She knew that tone. Could see the look in his eye, and everything within her screamed "danger." She cleared her suddenly tight throat. "With a rag and water."

"Then I really do need that bath."

"Very well. If you insist."

"I do. And do you know how to read?" he asked, cocking his head to the side. How soon he had gone from vulnerable patient to roguish charmer.

"Of course I can read," she said in a tone that implied the question was silly. She knew that many servants were uneducated, so he would probably assume she was no different. "What do you wish me to read?"

22

"Byron, perhaps? Or Shelley?"

Of course he would like Byron. The two shared so many similar characteristics, after all. "I shall check your brother's library and see what I can find."

"Thank you, Shannon. You are far too kind."

She liked his voice, and the way he said her name. He was so beautiful it was difficult not to stare. It was one thing to look at him when he was sleeping and unaware, but when he was staring at her so intently, and right after she'd seen him perform the most intimate of acts, it felt strange.

So disturbingly strange she looked away.

"I will see to your dinner now. That is, if you'll be all right without me. Perhaps I should call for someone to watch over you?"

He walked toward her, the sheet hanging dangerously low where he'd tied it at his waist. She held her breath, just waiting for it to drop.

He was two steps away from her when he wavered on his feet. Shannon reached out to settle him and would have ended up on her bottom if it weren't for the bed. Her breath left her in a rush as his full weight landed on top of her. Every solid inch of his powerful body covered her. She pushed against his shoulder, but he didn't budge.

Oh, for God's sake.

"My lord," she said urgently, pushing against him, but he didn't move. However, she felt the hard ridge of his cock pressing into her belly.

Much to her horror, the blood in her veins simmered, pooling low in her groin. Even her nipples tightened. Her nose was buried in his neck and she inhaled deeply. Thank goodness reality came in the way of a familiar scent. Jasmine. Candice's perfume.

"Rory!" she said, her voice firm, trying without success to squeeze out from beneath him.

Slowly, his eyes fluttered open and he stared down at her, his brows furrowing as though he were trying to figure out how she had gotten there.

She shifted, and the sides of his mouth lifted in a scandalously handsome smile. Was it her imagination, or had his manhood become even harder? He made a moaning sound, and his long hair tickled her shoulder and face. Why did she suddenly feel the desire to bury her head in those tresses?

"What happened?" he asked, his gaze fastening on her lips.

Oh dear.

"You lost consciousness," she said, her face turning hot. "I tried to steady you . . . but we fell onto the bed, and I have tried without success to move you. I have been trying to wake you." Dear God, she was babbling like an idiot.

He laughed under his breath.

What the hell? "It is not funny. You are not well. You are pale and sweaty, and I fear a fever might have taken hold. For your information, fevers could be deadly in this situation." Now why had she said that?

Was it her imagination, or had he shifted his hips and applied more pressure on her nether regions? Yes, there was no denying the hard-as-stone ridge of his manhood resting snug against her mound.

Lord help her, but she had the most insane desire to spread her legs wide and arch against him. What would it feel like to have him buried deep inside her, this man who had been making love to another woman scant minutes before?

He took his weight off her chest by propping himself up on his elbows. At least she wasn't being crushed and could perhaps start thinking clearly.

He stared down at her, his face inches from hers. Good God, he was so perfect it almost hurt to look at him.

Still supporting his own weight, he continued to watch her. His thumbs brushed gently across her temples. "You are so striking with your pale hair and eyes. And incredibly delicate. I feel like you could break if I am not careful."

Well, apparently he wasn't *that* concerned, because he wasn't budging.

An image of him and Candice flashed before her eyes and she frowned. "You're crushing me." She gave him one final shove.

Something that resembled disappointment flashed in his eyes before he rolled off of her and onto his back. Thank God the sheet was still draped about his waist, but it did little to hide his enormous erection.

She slid off the bed, straightened her skirts, and cleared her throat. "I-I shall return shortly."

4

Rory sat forward in the bath as Shannon washed his broad back. She had spoon-fed him broth, insisting he finish the entire bowlful before he stepped foot in the water, and he had done so, if only to pacify her. He had absolutely no appetite, but he enjoyed her care and attention too much to deny her. And she took her duty quite seriously.

"Where are you from, Shannon?" he asked, and he felt her stiffen.

"Scotland."

Little liar. He had heard the Irish brogue slip through more than once in their conversations. "Where in Scotland?"

"A small village near Inverness," she said, sounding uncomfortable with the discussion.

"Why did you leave?"

"There was more opportunity in London."

He could hardly argue with that. "What of your family?"

"Dead."

Perhaps that's where her hesitation came from. Suddenly, he felt guilty for pushing her.

"I'm sorry."

She began soaping his hair vigorously, her nails scraping his scalp. Honestly, he enjoyed the feel of her touching him, even if she was being a bit rough. He smiled inwardly and remembered the feel of her body beneath him when they'd fallen onto the bed, the soft mounds of her breasts pressed against his chest, the way his cock had nestled between the juncture of her thighs. If he hadn't been mistaken, she'd lifted her hips just the slightest bit too.

He wondered if she could read minds, because she abruptly dumped a pitcher of water over his head without warning him.

Wiping his hands down his face, he looked at her with brow furrowed. "You could have forewarned me, you know?"

He glanced down at the now wet dressing.

"I'm so sorry. I thought I did," she said sweetly.

Too sweetly.

He shook his head. "No, you didn't."

Her gaze shifted to the top of his head. "Ye still have suds in your hair, my lord."

Ah, she'd slipped again with the brogue. He watched her closely, gauging her reaction to see if she realized that she'd done as much, and her cheeks turned pink. But was the blush because of the slipup or because he was staring at her? She had such fragile features, perfectly sculpted, and he loved the way her top lip curved upward. Lord, but how he wanted to taste those lips.

She looked away and abruptly moved directly behind him. Dipping the pitcher in the tub, her hand came very close to his buttocks. He glanced over his shoulder and saw her gaze fasten on his lower back.

He grinned. She might pretend indifference, but he could sense interest. He wondered if she had any experience at all.

The majority of the women he'd been with knew their way around the bedchamber, but he had a feeling Shannon was as innocent as she looked.

Letting his head fall back on his shoulders, he closed his eyes. "All right, I'm ready."

This time she didn't dump, but rather poured the water slowly, the fingers of her free hand sliding through his hair.

Shannon wondered how many women would envy her position right now. To have Lord Ambrose naked in a tub, weak and defenseless, was a novelty, and one she was enjoying far too much for her own good.

And now at least all traces of his liaison with Candice had been washed away. The servant had been talking with her husband when Shannon had walked into the kitchen and ordered the soup and a bath. Frank had even inquired about his lordship's health.

Candice, wearing a fresh new uniform, was doing everything to change the subject.

Frank had kissed her affectionately on the cheek, and Shannon had to walk away. She hated deceit in every way. Her mother had been a loyal wife to her father and her father loyal in return. Loyalty and trust were qualities that would always be very important to her.

Loyalty and trust were not attributes of this particular Rayborne brother, who was better known for his activities in the bedchamber and who he'd killed on the dueling field, over anything of merit.

"My lord, do you make it a habit of sleeping with other men's wives?" Her eyes widened when she realized she'd said the words aloud.

Rory settled back against the tub's edge. "Yes, I suppose I do."

She frowned, surprised he'd admitted as much. "Why, when a man such as you could never be in short supply of a willing woman?"

He shrugged. "I suppose being with a married woman is just easier and less complicated."

What kind of an answer was that? "How could being with another man's wife possibly be easier and less complicated? Do you not feel in the least bit guilty knowing that you are helping that person break a vow?"

His brow furrowed as though he was really contemplating the matter, and after a few moments, he said, "Actually, I don't. I am not married, so it need not bother my conscience."

He truly was a devil. Completely insufferable. "Not in the least bit?"

He shrugged. "Not in the least bit."

"What if your wife were to do the same to you?"

His blue eyes narrowed as though the very idea were preposterous. "First off, I would *never* marry a woman who would be unfaithful."

She could not keep the smile from her lips. Did he honestly believe that he could control such a thing?

"Do I humor you, Shannon?" he asked, his dark brow lifted high.

"Forgive me for my impertinence, my lord, but how would you know if your wife were unfaithful? Unless you noted her every move, she could possibly be seeing someone else behind your back."

"I would know," he said matter-of-factly.

Just because he was a master at deceit, didn't mean he would recognize an unfaithful wife's sins. "I think you are far too confident, my lord. For all those husbands you have cuckolded, you could very well find yourself in the same position one day."

30

He eased farther down into the water, and she forced her gaze away from his impressive anatomy. "You can say whatever you wish, Shannon, but when I marry, it will be to a woman with a sterling reputation."

She refrained from rolling her eyes. "Of course. God forbid that your wife ask the same of you in return," she said, tossing the rag at him.

"I'm too tired to bathe myself," he said, handing the rag back to her.

He was worse than a child. "I will not bathe you when you are clearly capable."

"Please," he said, his voice both urgent and needy.

With an exaggerated sigh, she lathered the rag with the wonderfully scented soap and began washing his chest and the muscled planes of his taut belly.

A strange excited feeling came over her. An unfamiliar sensation, and she tried with all her might to wish it away.

She skipped over his anatomy and went to work on his legs. He yawned and she was happy to see he was getting tired again. Hopefully he would fall asleep before he demanded she read to him. After the past hour especially, she felt the need to be as far away from him as possible.

If it wasn't for the fact her responsibilities of caring for him excused her from her usual duties, then she would have asked another maid to take her place. But she had enjoyed the freedom this position afforded her, and truth be told, there were worse things than watching over a wealthy, handsome lord. Even if that wealthy, handsome lord was arrogant to a fault and a dangerous rakehell to boot.

She finished washing his feet, between his toes, and then stood. Reaching for the towel, she lifted it up, effectively hiding his body from her. "Step out, please," she said, turning her head away.

She could feel his gaze on her. Was he smirking at her?

Biting her lip, lest she say something she regret, she proceeded to dry him off, trying all the while not to think how absolutely delightful he smelled. The oils she had used in the bath water to ease his body aches smelled heavenly, and mixed with his own musky scent, they made her want to sigh. And even more, the oils made the water droplets cling to his lovely olive skin.

She swallowed past the tightness in her throat as she dried his strong back, the high curve of his buttocks, and his long, muscular legs.

Before she finished, he turned, his cock full in her face, and it was not flaccid. Indeed, it jutted proudly from the nest of dark hair.

Her pulse skittered.

Standing abruptly, she pushed the towel into his hands and stepped toward the bed, pulling down the sheets.

He approached the bed, and she felt like taking a step back for every one he took forward. He unsettled her like no one else.

Tossing the towel aside, he knelt on the bed and then flopped onto his back with a sigh. Not bothering to cover his loins, he winced as he touched his wound.

Her cheeks burned, much as the blood within her veins. An unfamiliar need coursed through her, making her feel alive in a way she'd never before experienced.

It was all his fault. How she wished he would convalesce somewhere else. Perhaps she would ask for another servant to tend to him, but then an image of him doing what he did to Candice, to one of the countless other maids in the household came to mind, and she knew she would endure.

You want him for yourself, an inner voice said.

It was true. . . . She *did* want Rory. Her body didn't lie.

He watched her, and she wondered if he knew the scandalous thoughts racing through her mind. She licked her lips and his gaze shifted to her mouth. When he met her gaze once more, his eyes looked darker, heavy-lidded.

Oh dear.

She yanked the sheet up past his firm belly, fluffed the pillow beside his head and then set about bandaging the wound. He stared at her, barely blinking, which made her exceedingly nervous.

It didn't take her long at all to finish her task, and with a final look at her workmanship, she made a move for the door.

"I thought you were going to read to me."

She cleared her throat. "I fear I forgot the book. Perhaps tomorrow. Plus, you need your rest anyway."

He turned his head and looked at her. "Go get the book, Shannon."

"But you are so tired. You can barely keep your eyes open," she said, in one final effort to change his mind.

His long lashes cast shadows upon his cheekbones. "I want you to read to me. I will not relent, so you may as well go get a book."

Her nails bit into her palms. He was so annoying! "It has been a trying day. Perhaps I can send someone else. I do believe Candice would be more to your liking."

"I want you." He said the words so matter-of-factly, it made her pause.

When she could once again think straight, she swallowed and inclined her head. "Very well, if you insist. I shall be right back."

She closed the door behind her and walked leisurely down the long hallway and down the stairs to the library. If she took her time, then it was her hope that he would fall asleep while she was gone, and she would not have to endure any more of his attitude for the rest of the evening.

The library had floor-to-ceiling mahogany bookcases stuffed full of tomes. Shannon had always loved reading as a child, and could spend an entire afternoon getting lost in another world. Since leaving Ireland she had not had the time to read. Being a servant, she had learned that one's time was not one's own, and she always fell into bed exhausted each night.

She ran across a copy of Robert Burns's latest poems and slipped it in a pocket. The grandfather clock in the corner ticked away the minutes. Indeed, she was surprised when she noted she'd been gone for a good half hour and decided she had dallied long enough.

Walking up the stairs, she realized how very tired, both mentally and physically, she had become.

She had known the servants her family had employed had been hardworking, but she'd never realized until now just how hardworking. If she ever saw them again, she would tell them just how much she appreciated their efforts.

She paused outside Rory's chamber door, hoping more than anything he would be snoring on the other side.

5

Shannon's heart plummeted.

Unfortunately, Rory was not asleep, but sitting beside the fire, wearing Lord Graston's silk robe that Edward had brought to him, along with other clothing just in case he "desired to get up and around."

He glanced at her as she shut the door. His dark hair was still not brushed, but she could tell he'd finger-combed the dark tresses back off his face, which only served to draw more emphasis to his striking features. He was like a Michelangelo statue brought to life.

"You should be in bed, my lord," she said, her voice sounding suspiciously husky.

"I'm tired of being in bed."

"But you only just woke up."

He shrugged. "Perhaps, but I want to sit now." His voice broached no argument, and he motioned to the chair across from him.

Playing the obedient servant, she sat down and opened the book. Clearing her throat, she began to read.

People said that some of Burns's poems were about his many lovers, and this particular one was about a woman named Jean.

"Have you ever had a lover, Shannon?"

She looked up from the book and laid her hand flat on the pages. "Excuse me?"

"Have you ever had a lover?" He said the words slowly, as though she were an idiot.

Her insides twisted. Never in her life had she been asked such an intimate question. "It's none of your business, my lord."

His brilliant blue eyes widened a little. "Ah, I've hit a nerve."

"I believe you are *trying* to unnerve me, my lord," she said, straightening her shoulders and lifting her chin high. She would not allow him to make her squirm.

He smiled wolfishly. "Perhaps I am."

Damn him for getting under her skin.

Edward appeared at the door, and Shannon was grateful for the interruption, though she was surprised she hadn't heard him. Rory glanced at him. "Yes, Edward?"

"My lord, you have a visitor. I told her that you were most likely sleeping, but she did not seem to care. I fear she's quite insistent on seeing you."

Her? Why should Shannon be surprised his first guest would be a woman?

His brow furrowed. "Might the woman in question be Lady Anna?"

"Indeed, my lord."

Rory gave an exaggerated sigh. "Well, I know she will not relent unless you show her up."

Shannon remembered the beautiful young woman coming to Lady Graston's townhouse to visit Marilyn. After her departure, a few of the servants had whispered about her scandalous reputation. They had said that she had many lovers, among them Lord Ambrose. Indeed, another said that she had made love to both Lord Graston and Lord Ambrose at the same time, but she could not see her master doing such a thing, even if it was before he met Lady Graston.

"I can serve her tea in the parlor until you are dressed and ready to receive her," Edward said. "Shall I assist you?"

"No, Shannon can assist me, and I am not up to leaving my chamber. I can receive Lady Anna here . . . but please give me a few moments first."

He was receiving Anna in his chamber? Lady Graston would be horrified, for she did everything by the book. Well, Shannon did not have to wonder why he wanted to receive Anna in his room. No doubt they would take up where they had left off.

What a scoundrel.

"Of course, my lord, if that is what you would prefer," Edward said, looking uncomfortable. "I will leave you in Shannon's capable hands."

Shannon could feel her cheeks turning hotter by the second and was relieved when the butler left the room. She wondered why she should even bother to help Rory dress when he would probably end up removing those clothes within seconds of Lady Anna entering the chamber anyway.

She walked to the wardrobe, opened the doors, and pulled out a freshly laundered shirt and a loose-fitting pair of trousers. Rory stood and dropped the robe. She swallowed hard, trying with difficulty to keep her gaze above his chin.

Good gracious, he was certainly proud of his body.

Mentally reciting the alphabet backward in an effort to avert her wicked thoughts, she had to balance on the tip of her toes to get the shirt over his head, a difficult task when she trembled like a leaf. He shook his head when it came to the drawers. Not questioning him, she assisted him with his trousers, and he grabbed her shoulder to keep steady. This, too, proved difficult considering she had to do the majority of the work. For the love of God, she knew he was weak, but how hard was it to lift one's leg?

Even worse, he made no move to button his trousers, and instead watched her with lifted brow. Did he think she wouldn't? Steadying her hands, she reached for the fastenings and managed to close the bottom two buttons.

"You might want to tuck in the shirt, else it will be too bulky once the trousers are fastened."

Nodding obediently, Shannon shoved the shirt tails in, her hands brushing over his bare buttocks. This was altogether too intimate. His masculine scent enveloped her, the heat of his body, the *strength* of his body when she touched him made her pulse quicken and her entire body feel flushed.

She buttoned his trousers and smiled triumphantly. "Would you like me to assist you with your stockings?"

"There is no need."

"Shall I brush your hair?"

"Yes. Where would you like me?"

"At the vanity, please."

He sat down on the small bench before the vanity, his long legs before him, which he crossed at the ankle. She stepped behind him and ran the brush through his dark, thick locks. He was watching her in the mirror . . . closely.

She refused to meet his gaze, afraid of what he might see in her eyes. No doubt he could tell when a woman wanted him. Was there a woman alive who didn't? Certainly she knew what it felt like to be admired. She'd had her share of suitors before her parents' death, but her father had been extremely protective. He felt that she was too young to be courted, despite the fact that he had begun courting her mother when she'd been just sixteen.

The door opened abruptly and Shannon turned to find Lady Anna, dressed in an exquisite turquoise gown with elegant lace trimmings. "Well, isn't this a lovely spectacle," she said coyly.

Rory stood and Shannon set the brush on the vanity.

"I thought you were waiting in the parlor," Rory said, hands on hips, looking not in the least surprised by the interruption.

Anna's lips quirked as she glanced from Rory to Shannon and back again. "When the butler went to get tea, I snuck up here to see how you were." Her gaze flicked to Shannon. "I now understand why you are convalescing at your brother's home instead of your parents' townhouse."

"Mother gave Sinjin and Katelyn the townhouse for a wedding present, and they are renovating it while they're away."

"So I realized when the servant opened the door. Katelyn, or Lady Mawbry, is a lovely woman, but I have to say after catching a brief glimpse of the new foyer, that I question her taste in décor."

"Careful, that is my brother's wife you speak of," Rory said in a cautionary tone.

Anna shrugged. "And she really might consider having the servants wear uniforms. The butler was dressed in a hideous suit from at least four seasons ago."

Her gaze slid slowly over Shannon. "What quaint little uniforms. See, now Lady Graston knows how to run a household efficiently. Lady Mawbry might take a few lessons from her. But then again, Lady Mawbry probably does not have such beautiful help."

The flirtatious manner of the other woman put Shannon on guard. And Lady Anna's mention of her being a servant only reminded Shannon of the day when she had worn beautiful, expensive gowns, much like the one Lady Anna now wore. Her mother had always enjoyed taking her shopping, and she had been allowed to buy what she wanted, when she wanted, with no thought of consequence. But those days were long behind her.

Shannon glanced at Rory and reached for the bowl of water she'd used to cool him earlier. "If you need anything, my lord, please let me know."

"Thank you, Shannon," he said, his eyes soft.

Anna's lips quirked as she watched them.

Shannon couldn't get out of the room fast enough, and she felt Rory's gaze on her the entire way to the door. As she exited, she could swear she heard the other woman laugh beneath her breath.

What a horrible, mean-spirited woman. If this was the company the young baron kept, then she would be wise to keep a distance from him in the future.

Cheeks burning, Shannon shut the door slowly, despite the fact she ached to slam it.

Rory turned to his guest. "So, what do I owe the pleasure of this visit?"

Anna's lips curved into a mischievous smile. "I heard that you had been injured, and I wanted to see for myself how you were faring."

"As you can see, I am alive."

"Thank God for that," she said in a silky-soft voice. "I had thought I had lost my lover for good."

He rolled his eyes and took a seat in the nearest chair, surprised at how tired he was from the bath. The lavender was quite effective.

"Plus, I have missed you."

"Missed me? Come, I've heard it on good authority that you are sleeping with a tailor on Bond Street. You couldn't miss me that much."

Her eyes widened. "Where on earth did you hear such a dastardly rumor, and one that could not be farther from the truth?"

"It's a lie?"

She shrugged, which essentially meant she was guilty. "Perhaps, but I did not come here to talk about me. I've come to see that you are well, and to tell you the latest."

Rory could not help but smile. She was not here because of concern for him, but rather she had gossip that involved him.

"It seems the newly widowed, thanks to you, Lady Cordland has gone on record that you are not only a scoundrel who seduced her, but a murderer to boot."

Rory flinched, shocked by the allegation.

"First off, she had her hand down my pants within seconds of our first greeting, and as to murder, I didn't pull the trigger until *after* her husband got a shot off. Unfortunately for him, he missed."

Her gaze shifted to his shoulder. "So says the rumor mill, but still, Rory, did you have to kill the man?"

Her tone was flippant and sarcastic, and Rory didn't appreciate it. He wasn't proud of the fact he'd killed anyone, and despite the fact the man had been a letch of the first order, Cordland's death would haunt him the rest of his days. "Where did you see Lady Cordland?"

"Actually, I didn't see her, but the duel was all that anyone could talk about at tea this afternoon. Lady Cordland's best friend was in attendance, and she is vigorously circulating the news, and naming you as the villain and she the victim."

"Let's face it . . . I did her a favor. Cordland was humiliating her by taking up with her cousin. Everyone knew it, and now she has license to take up with as many lovers as she chooses."

Anna sighed heavily, as though she truly cared. "This will probably ruin her. You know, she did have an excellent reputation before you got a hold of her."

"Are you trying to make me feel worse than I already do?"

Her mouth dropped open. "Of course not. I just wanted to share the news, and let you know what is being said about you. Plus, I missed your company. There is no one else in London who makes me laugh the way you can." She walked toward him and leaned in, her hands sliding up his thighs. "Not to mention, you are one of the best lovers I've ever had."

"*One* of the best?"

"All right, the best," she said, kissing his cheek. "Though I admit, Victor could come in as a tie."

Anna and he had been lovers for some time, and though they were far from monogamous, they did have a certain compatibility that worked for them. But oddly, even as he thought about making love to Anna, he saw Shannon's face.

"I am exhausted," he said before he could stop himself.

She laughed loudly. "My God, the little servant has gotten under your skin."

Was it that obvious?

"I haven't touched her."

The smile disappeared from her face. "But you want to."

Yes, he did . . . desperately. But he didn't want Anna knowing any more than she did already, especially since she was incapable of keeping a secret. "So, why did you really come here, Anna, aside from being the bearer of bad news, that is?" He was wise enough to know she had more on her mind than just sex.

She straightened, lifted her chin, and looked him in the eye. "I understand Lady Graston is having a soiree very soon."

"Yes, a housewarming of sorts."

"I had not received an invitation and I was hoping you could speak with her on my behalf."

"Why do you wish to attend?"

She licked her lips. "Let's just say that there is someone who I would very much like to see."

There was a rare vulnerability in her eyes that surprised him, and he knew immediately whom she spoke of. "And would that certain someone happen to be related to Lady Graston?"

"Rory, you are too wise for your own good."

"Correct me if I am wrong, but I recently helped you gain an audience with Marilyn, and that did not go at all well, from what I understand."

The smile faded from her lips. "Perhaps time has changed her way of thinking."

Her expression had changed, and he could tell he had struck a nerve. "Marilyn is engaged, Anna. Let her be."

"I cannot let her be," she said abruptly, dropping her hands back to her sides. "I don't like how we left things. I just want the opportunity to talk to her."

Anna's reputation was slowly coming unraveled, but rather than save herself, she went out of her way to cause scandal. Sadly, there was little he could do to help her, save remain her friend and confidante. "Very well, I shall speak to Lily, and if she agrees and you do attend the soiree, you are not allowed to make a scene."

Her grin returned in force. "Thank you. What a dear friend you are. I promise you that I shall be as good as gold."

6

Shannon tried without success to keep from thinking of what might be happening in the guest chamber between her patient and his visitor. And she was not the only one. She heard two of the housekeepers speculating as well. They'd fallen silent when Shannon had come across them gossiping in the parlor.

Certainly Lord Ambrose would not make love to yet another woman on the same day, would he?

Given his reputation, she could hardly put anything past him.

And damn her body. It betrayed her every single time she thought of being pinned beneath his powerful frame. She still burned for him, wanted to feel those large hands on her, wanted to experience what it was all those other women had. Those lucky, lucky women.

She tried to clear her thoughts as she approached an attractive footman, who nodded in greeting. Not much older than herself, he had dark brown eyes framed by long lashes and curly chestnut hair. Whenever they served the evening meal together, she could feel his gaze on her. "How are ye today, Shannon?" he asked in a thick Scottish accent.

"Very well, Johnny, and you?"

"Better now, thank ye, lass," he said with a wink, and Shannon immediately dropped her gaze.

"Can I get that for ye?" He motioned to the large bowl of water she carried.

"No, I have it. Thank you, though." She shifted on her feet, feeling increasingly awkward. "Well, I should get back to work."

"I'll see ye later."

"Yes, I'll see you later." She continued walking, needing a breath of fresh air, anything to get out of the house and clear her head from thoughts of the sinfully handsome lord who seemed to invade even her dreams of late.

The door was already ajar, and she pushed it open with a nudge. She threw the water out onto the grass and noticed a man standing near the hedge, looking at her.

Her breath caught in her throat. Was he watching the house? Of average height, he had a stocky build. He was also middle-aged and had gray hair and a thick mustache. Oh dear God, was this the same man whom Zachary had seen?

It had to be.

Dressed in a heavy black coat and a top hat, he took a step closer to the hedge, then turned and disappeared into the thicket of trees.

With her heart racing, she darted back inside the manor, rushed down the hallway, and into the parlor that was lined with windows. Crossing the room, she went to the last window, slid the drape aside, and glanced out.

She scanned the trees, her heart leaping nearly from her chest when she caught sight of him rushing toward the main road.

She had to talk to Zachary.

Forcing herself not to run, she made her way to the stables

and found him brushing down a horse. There was another groom in an adjacent stall, so she had to be careful.

Zachary glanced up at her, his surprise evident. "Shannon, what are you doing?"

"I—" she stopped short, remembering their last conversation about leaving if they saw the man again.

The thought of running again made her ill at ease. She felt so secure with Lord and Lady Graston, and the very idea of looking for work in another town was downright depressing. "I wanted to tell you that Cook made bread pudding, and I thought perhaps you would like some."

He seemed to visibly relax. "Cook would have my head if I snuck bread pudding from her kitchen. You know that, Shannon."

She did know that, and now she wished she had not rushed out to the stables. "Well, I should be returning before Edward discovers I am missing."

Zachary tilted his head to the side, his eyes narrowing. "Is there something else that's bothering you, Shannon?"

"No, I just wanted a break from the manor."

He followed her outside.

"Well, I can certainly understand that, especially since you've been caring for his lordship's brother."

She hoped he could not see the desire she felt for Rory in her eyes. Flustered, she lifted her face to the sun and took a deep breath. "It feels so good to breathe the fresh air."

"I imagine it does. I'm so grateful I get to work out-of-doors."

She glanced at him, considering the repercussions of not saying anything to him about the strange man. "Well, I should return. I shall see you later."

"All right."

She walked away, knowing that if he ever discovered the

truth that she had seen the man they assumed was their cousin's henchman, then he would be furious.

Entering the house, her thoughts were in turmoil. Perhaps she should go back to Zachary and tell him the truth?

"Shannon, there you are," Edward said, looking at the empty bowl in her hands. "I wondered where you went off to when I served tea to Lord Ambrose and Lady Anna."

"To get fresh water," she said absently, heading off to do just that.

When she'd refilled the water bowl, she walked down the hallway, dreading to return to Rory and his guest.

She turned the corner and walked up the steps, and nearly ran straight into Lady Anna. The water spilled over the edge and onto Shannon's gown, dousing the stomach area. Thank goodness for the apron, and thank goodness the water had not ended up on Lady Anna instead.

Lady Anna put her hand on Shannon's shoulder. "You are such a lovely little thing, aren't you?" Her dark eyes narrowed slightly, her gaze shifting to Shannon's lips. "I could just eat you up."

What an odd thing to say.

"Excuse me, my lady," Shannon said, sidestepping Lady Anna, anxious to be away from her.

Before she knew it, she stood at Rory's chamber door. Taking a deep breath, she opened the door and breathed a sigh of relief.

He was asleep.

Clinton O'Connor paced the rough wood floor where he'd been staying for the past fortnight. For months now he'd hoped for a break in finding his cousins, and finally, with the help of Jacob, one of Dublin's finest investigators, he had them cornered.

Zachary and Shannon were somewhere in London, or so the note had said. Jacob had lost the boy once, but this latest note had fueled his hopes, and he felt their luck had changed.

He had faith in Jacob. The older man was like a bloodhound. And even more, Jacob believed Clinton when he said his cousins were responsible for the fire. That belief was a welcome change. In Dublin, he had seen the looks in people's eyes when he walked past. Suspicion. He was the only living heir to the O'Connor dynasty, and the family had been wiped out by a fire, and yet he had remained untouched. His excuse had been that he'd gone hunting, and he had an alibi in one of the O'Connor's servants. A lad who owed him a veritable fortune in gambling debts.

That alibi had silenced a few, including the magistrate, but he still knew that many wondered about his involvement.

Glancing at the clock on the mantel, he cursed under his breath. Jacob was supposed to meet him over an hour ago. Had Shannon and Zachary managed to slip through his fingers yet again?

Damn them! If only they had perished in that fire, then he would not have to worry about them popping up down the road and ruining everything. As it was, he'd taken control of his uncle's business. He had played the grieving nephew to perfection, even gaining a fiancée, Gwendolyn, the daughter of his uncle's pompous solicitor. She was the prize of the season, and he'd been thrilled to win her hand. Unfortunately, the more time he'd spent with her, the more irksome he found her. And good Lord, the woman shopped like there was no tomorrow. He was terrified at what awaited him after the vows were exchanged.

He heard footsteps in the hallway and stopped pacing. Three light taps came on the door, and he rushed to open it. "Come in, Jacob."

Jacob swept the hat from his head and entered. As always, he never turned his back to Clinton and stayed close to the door.

"What news?"

"I have located them, sir."

Exhilaration rushed along Clinton's spine. It was the news he'd been waiting for. "Did you see them?"

"Yes, the girl works in the house, and the boy works in the stables."

It was the closest they had ever come, and he could scarcely believe that soon all his dreams were within reach. "Excellent work, Jacob. I am well pleased." With his heart pumping nearly out of his chest, he walked toward the dresser and removed a roll of notes. "Here ye are as promised. I shall give ye the rest when I confirm that it is indeed them."

Jacob flipped through the notes, obviously satisfied, he shoved them into his pocket.

"Neither one saw you, did they?" Clinton asked, and the other man shook his head.

"No, sir. They are at Lord and Lady Graston's manor in Twickenham. The estate borders the River Thames. I should warn ye that it is difficult to get on the grounds, or near the grounds, without being noticed. The place is swarming with servants."

"Have no fear. I shall find a way in."

"Ye know where to find me if ye need me, sir," Jacob said, hand already on the doorknob.

"Very well. Thank you for your hard work."

"You're welcome, sir."

Jacob left. Clinton shut the door behind him and smiled.

Shannon and Zachary would soon be dead, and there would be nothing standing in his way and the future he had always dreamed of.

7

"He has been asking for you all day, my dear. Why do you not go to him?"

Shannon brushed a curl out of her face and glanced at the servant who had been so kind as to tend to Rory for her today.

When she didn't respond, the older woman with a kind smile and gentle spirit patted Shannon on the back. "He seems quite taken with you, my dear. Perhaps you should go to him and set his mind at ease."

"He needs his rest, and I think he enjoys making me squirm."

Helda's lips quirked. "If I were young, I could certainly understand why he would make a woman squirm, but alas, I have sons older than him."

Shannon smiled for the first time all day. She had stayed with Rory last night and awoke before dawn in the chair beside the bed. In her dreams she had been kissing him, her hands moving over his strong body, the wide chest, the chiseled abdomen, and the long, thick length of his sex. She had awoken with her heart pounding and her blood on fire. Trying to catch her breath, she'd looked over at her patient to find his hand shoved beneath the sheets, covering his impressive cock. Her mouth had gone dry, and she stood on unsteady legs, and headed straight for the door. She never looked back. How could she look at him without reliving that dream all over again?

"Just check in on him, my dear."

"Would you mind serving him dinner?" she asked, and Helda frowned.

"He will be heartily disappointed when I walk in and it's not you."

Shannon glanced past Helda and her eyes widened. Rory was walking down the stairs, dressed in a handsome gray suit and snowy white shirt that only served to accent his dark, good looks. Polished knee-high black boots finished off the ensemble. He was strikingly handsome, and there wasn't a woman alive who would deny him.

Not even her.

The old servant gave her a wink and then rushed off down the hall.

Had he heard any part of their discussion?

"Shannon," he said tersely.

"You are leaving?" Shannon asked, surprised at how much distress the thought of him walking out the door made her feel.

He lifted a dark brow. "Where were you all day?"

"I had other duties to attend to, and I wanted you to rest." Why was it she felt so guilty for steering clear of him?

Outside, she heard the carriage being brought around. "Do you think it is a good idea to leave? I mean—when you are not yet fully recovered? What if you have a fever?" She absolutely resisted the temptation to feel his forehead, even though she yearned to.

His brows furrowed and the side of his mouth curved in an

exasperated smile. "Shannon, you are sounding like my mother now."

Sounding like his mother certainly was not her intention, and she felt her cheeks grow hot in embarrassment. Worse still, thoughts of her wicked dream came back to haunt her, and she dropped her gaze between them. "Forgive me, my lord. . . . I was just concerned about your injury."

"You need not remind me of my wound, Shannon. I feel it every time I draw breath."

It hurt him to breathe and yet he was going out? What sense did that make? "And when will you be returning, my lord?"

Checking his appearance in the mirror above a side table, he said, "I cannot say for certain, only that I plan on returning. But do not wait up, or rather, have whomever you are pawning me off on wait up."

"I did not pawn you off."

"Shannon, you've avoided me all day, and now you cannot even meet my gaze. Apparently I said something to offend you."

Now she just felt stupid and childish. She hated the thought of him walking out the door. He had brought a certain spark into her life that had been long missing.

When she said nothing, he shook his head. "I must go," he said, walking in long strides toward the door.

She could only imagine him striding into a soiree and having every head turn. Would he still be leaving if she had stayed to take care of him? she wondered.

Fighting the jealousy that threatened to consume her, she forced a smile. "Have a lovely evening, my lord."

"Thank you, Shannon," he replied, and opened the door.

Johnny was dressed in dark tails. "Are ye ready, my lord?"

"Indeed, I am," Rory replied.

Seeing her, Johnny grinned widely. "Good evening, Shannon."

Rory caught the exchange and his jaw clenched. "Come, boy."

Johnny's gaze shifted over her slowly, before he walked down the steps.

Rory glanced at her one final time before walking out the door. His blue eyes were so intense, she shifted on her feet. How she wished she could dress up in her finery and have her hair coiffed in the latest styles. What would he say if he saw her like that? Would he pass her by, or would he stop dead in his tracks?

It didn't matter. She would never know. She was an impoverished servant now, not the daughter of one of Ireland's wealthiest businessmen and one of Dublin's most sought-after debutantes.

Rory tried to enjoy himself, but it was bloody hard when his thoughts kept returning to a certain blonde with ice-blue eyes and a fiery attitude.

Truth be told, he quite liked that Shannon wasn't the quiet, demure girl he had met weeks ago at Lillith's townhouse in London. However, he had felt more than a little spurned when she had sent someone else to care for him. Was he so vexing that she could not tolerate his presence?

Setting back against the velvet cushions of the carriage, he considered having the groomsman turn back around. He had remembered Anna's invitation to drop by a small soiree in the heart of London and thought it sounded enjoyable. Yet, why did he suddenly wish he was back at his brother's home, lying on the bed, Shannon in a nearby chair reading to him?

He closed his eyes for just an instant, and when he opened them next, the coachman was peering in at him. "We are here, my lord."

Rory pulled back the lace curtain and stared up at the Georgian manor. Perhaps he would stay just a little while, see Anna, and assure everyone he was alive and well. Then he'd be on his way, back to Twickenham, and back to Shannon.

From the moment he entered the parlor, Rory was greeted by a bevy of friends and acquaintances, all excited to see him, their gaze directed in the vicinity of his shoulder.

Anna made her way to his side immediately, and he was actually glad to see his friend. "I cannot believe you came."

"Nor can I," he murmured, his shoulder killing him. "Can we sit somewhere?"

"Well, of course. Come."

Rory sat next to Anna on a horribly uncomfortable settee. He saw Thomas Lehman from the corner of his eye and he shifted in his seat, trying to forget about the ménage à trois he'd had with the other man and Anna. The blonde nodded at Rory, and he smiled back tightly and quickly looked away.

"He is dying to share your bed again," Anna whispered under her breath.

"I'm not interested," he said, taking a glass of wine from the servant's tray. He took a sip and nearly spit the warm spirits back into the glass. Instead, he swallowed.

A tall, young man with auburn hair and green eyes handed Rory a glass. "Whiskey, which is far better than what they're trying to pass off, quite unconvincingly, as wine."

Rory smiled. "Thank you."

"Clinton O'Connor," he said, extending a hand.

"Rory Rayborne, Lord Ambrose, and this is—"

"Lady Anna." Clinton took Anna's hand and brought it to his lips. "Yes, I've already been fortunate enough to meet the most beautiful woman in the room."

"Mr. O'Connor has come to London on business," Anna said with a lazy smile, sliding her hand from the man's grasp.

Clinton rolled back on his heels. "I met our host at White's last night, and he was kind enough to invite me to tonight's festivities."

Although he was trying a bit too hard to charm, Clinton O'Connor proved to be a quick-witted companion, one that Anna seemed genuinely interested in, and he, in turn, seemed intrigued by her as well. Rory barely had to add to the conversation at all.

Lady Cordland's good friend saw Rory. Her eyes narrowed and she walked off in the other direction.

"That's not exactly the reaction I was hoping for," he said under his breath. At least the whiskey was warming his insides, and already the throbbing in his shoulder was starting to subside.

"Will you be joining us for a drink at Mr. Lehman's later?" Clinton asked, and Rory shook his head. "I think not."

Anna frowned. "Oh, come, Rory. It is not like you to pass up such an opportunity."

His thoughts turned to a beautiful blonde servant with pale blue eyes. Why was it that he couldn't shake her from his thoughts for even a little while? Though he was tired, and he knew it was in his best interest to return to his brother's home, he said, "Very well, perhaps I shall."

Rory told himself to go home, even when he walked into the very small, very intimate "party" an hour later. He'd drunk far too much for someone in his condition, and though he could no longer feel his wound, his head pounded in time with his heartbeat.

Worse still, he didn't like the way Thomas Lehman was staring at him, like a plump goose on Christmas morning. It was all a little too disconcerting.

Anna handed him a tall glass of whiskey and sat so close their thighs touched. They had fallen into an easy relationship since Claymoore Hall, and he'd enjoyed their liaisons, but now he was not inclined to continue said relationship.

"Slip into the study with me?" Anna murmured in his ear.

"I think not," he said, stunned that his cock did not even stir.

Anna reared back a little, her brows furrowing. "What is this?"

"You forget I am wounded, Anna."

"Since when did that stop you?"

"I've never been on the receiving end of a bullet before. It has a way of interfering with one's most base instincts."

"Indeed, I hope I never experience such a thing."

"Being that you are a female, I think it is safe to say you should not be in danger of such an occurrence. If ever you do, however, find yourself facing an opponent with a pistol, just be sure to dodge the bullet."

"Excellent advice," Anna said with a wink.

"I thought your new little friend was coming," Thomas said to Anna, lighting his cigar with an oil lamp.

"Clinton will be here soon," Anna replied, glancing at Rory again. "And that is another reason you must stay. He liked you, and I think you should befriend him."

"You think I should befriend him?" Now it was his turn to frown. "I am not a child, and you are sounding more and more like my mother." First Shannon, now Anna.

Anna laughed. "You never liked being told what to do."

She leaned in and nibbled at his ear, a tactic that always made his blood turn hot.

Thomas stood and walked toward them, the look in his eye unmistakable.

Rory jumped to his feet. "Well, I hate to leave this little party, but I am exhausted and my wound is throbbing."

Anna lifted a brow.

"Are you sure you can't stay?" Thomas said, looking disappointed.

"I can't. I shall see you both soon, I'm certain," he said, walking in long strides to the door. A wave of dizziness rushed through him and he gripped the iron railing as he hailed for the carriage to be brought around.

Sweat beaded his forehead, and he reached into his pocket to wipe the kerchief against his brow. Good God, he was even trembling.

8

Rory returned at just around two A.M. Shannon had been unable to sleep, and had sighed with relief when she heard the carriage pull into the gravel drive.

She threw on a wrap and, lighting a candle, walked down the narrow servants' staircase to the next landing where the guest rooms were located.

The door to Rory's chamber was ajar, and Shannon knocked lightly, her hand on the knob. When no answer came, she pushed the door open and walked in.

Her heart gave a sharp jolt seeing Rory lying sideways on the bed, facedown. He had not bothered to remove his boots, or any other clothing, beyond his coat, cravat, and shirt—all items that were tossed haphazardly on the floor.

Shannon cleared her throat, but he did not so much as move.

To her relief, she saw that he was at least breathing, his back rising and falling—and good God, was he snoring?

She tugged at a boot and it came off easily enough. The other was a bit harder to remove, and Rory groaned as she yanked hard. The boot gave, but not without effort, and she very nearly ended up on her backside on the rug beneath her feet.

Setting the boots aside, she looked at Rory and contemplated leaving him as he was. That is, until she noticed the blood stain on the blanket beneath him.

She gasped, deeply concerned that he had disturbed the injury. Or what if this was a new wound? Given his reputation, she couldn't put anything past him.

Nudging him, she hoped he would roll over, but he didn't budge. Perhaps she should wake Zachary? But her brother would have to rise in a few hours to begin his day, and she knew that, like her, he struggled with falling and staying asleep. She shouldn't disrupt him because Lord Ambrose was so inebriated he was in danger of smothering himself.

Walking around the side of the bed where his head lay, she nudged his face to the side, so at least he could breathe. He exhaled and she choked on a breath. He smelled like liquor. Dear Lord, had he bathed in it?

When he didn't move, she got up on the bed and kneeled beside him. Reaching over him, she slid her hands along his ribs and pulled him toward her.

An agonizing moan escaped his lips as he rolled over and she gasped, seeing the wound had lost its dressing. No wonder the sheets had been bloody. She leaned close and felt guilty seeing how red and angry the skin appeared. There didn't seem to be any pus, but he would have to be extremely careful these next few days.

She would stay by his side day and night.

Edward had left a ceramic bowl full of water on the side table, along with soft cloths. Shannon soaked a cloth, then squeezed off the excess water, before gently wiping the wound.

She was sliding the rag along the reddened edges when he

reached up and grasped her arm. "What are you doing?" His words were slightly slurred.

She gasped, stunned by the pressure. "Rory, it's me. Shannon."

His eyes focused on her and his hold on her relaxed.

"The wound is bleeding. I need to dress it."

He nodded and closed his eyes. "Dear sweet, innocent Shannon."

Sweet and innocent. Was he taunting her?

She slid off the bed and went to the drawer where she had placed her supplies. He remained completely still as she approached.

"Perhaps you might want to lay straight on the bed," she urged.

"I don't want to move."

Which meant she had to climb back on the bed with him.

"Very well," she replied, kicking off her shoes and getting up on the bed again. She set the dressing aside and opened the salve that would help speed the healing.

She dipped a finger into the pot and then coated the wound liberally.

"Bloody hell, that hurts," he said between clenched teeth.

She was shocked he could feel anything, given he was so inebriated. "I am sorry, but the salve will help heal the wound. The physician left instructions."

"How would you know what the physician said? You weren't here when he came by earlier." His eyes were open, and he seemed more alert than before. Had it been an act? she wondered.

She chose to ignore the last statement. "I am surprised the dressing came off."

"That's what you get for leaving me to my own devices." He smiled, flashing white teeth, and her heart skipped a beat. "Actually, you can set your mind at ease. I did not yank it off, but rather Lady Anna was curious and asked to see the wound."

Shannon stopped in mid-motion. She could very well imagine how and why Lady Anna would remove his dressing. No wonder he had been so adamant about going out tonight. "Well, I suggest you, or your *friends*, refrain from taking off the bandage in the future. You do not need to risk infection. As it is, you are still in danger of fever."

He sighed heavily, his wide chest expanding. She tried to ignore the warm tendrils that wove their way through her stomach as her gaze shifted to the muscled planes of his abdomen and the dark line of hair that escaped beneath the band of his trousers. Her gaze abruptly returned to the task at hand.

She could feel him watch her. Sweat beaded her brow as desire made her nipples harden and the flesh between her thighs damp. "I should change the sheets. There is blood." Her voice came out huskier than usual, and she cleared her throat, hoping he did not catch the slight inflection.

"I can sit up and make your task easier," he said, wincing as he sat up on his elbows.

Her hands trembled as she continued with her task. It was so very difficult to keep focused on what she was doing when he was near. Had he shifted, or was she pressing into him, her upper body flush against his arm?

She met his gaze, and her breath lodged in her throat as he leaned toward her.

He kissed her, his lips light, soft, gentle.

For a split second her mind rebelled, but ultimately she kissed him back . . . and it was wonderful. He tasted like brandy and, oddly, mint.

"I've wanted you from the first moment I saw you," he whispered against her mouth. "You are so beautiful."

The acknowledgment that he wanted her made her pulse leap.

What was she supposed to say in response? She had never been so intimate with a man, and despite the obvious danger she was in, she could not pull away to save her life.

He leaned into her; then he was nudging her back onto the pillows. Her heart was a roar in her ears as her arms looped around his neck. She clung to him as he covered her with his body.

Desire licked at her spine, and as he deepened the kiss, the further enthralled she became and the more she wanted him. He lowered his head, kissed her throat, her neck, and the pulse that beat wildly.

He touched her breast, his fingers toying with a nipple, and her breath caught in her throat at the exquisite sensations rippling through her. There seemed to be an invisible thread between her breasts and her women's flesh, because with each tug, she felt the need to lift her hips, craving friction. Suddenly, he was pulling the neck of her gown down, his breath hot on the soft slopes of her breasts. He kissed one nipple, then the other, licking them, grazing them with his teeth in a way that made her cry out in ecstasy.

He used his knees to spread her thighs and settled between them, his thick cock pressing against her moist heat.

She rolled her hips and he moaned deep in his throat, a wonderful sound she knew she'd never forget. Desire teased every nerve ending, and she pressed closer against him, craving his touch.

He made a slight movement, and to her shock, her wrap was beneath her, and he was untying the thin ribbon of her chemise.

Before she could protest, he slid the garment over her head, and she lay naked beneath him. He looked down at her breasts, cupped one with his hand, and eased onto his side to look down at her, his gaze shifting to her mound and the pale curls there. "Beautiful," he said again, and he made her believe it, despite the fact he'd no doubt seen hundreds of naked women in his time.

Soon she was beyond thinking. His hands seemed to be everywhere at once, and his fingertips teased her nipples into firm peaks, while the other hand brushed over her stomach. It seemed an eternity before he touched her most intimate place, sliding a finger inside her.

Rory had never had a virgin before, and Shannon was clearly very much untouched, her tight inner muscles clenching his finger. He was shocked by her heated response, by the way she lifted her hips against his hand, seeking more contact.

His thumb brushed over her clit and she gasped, and even stopped kissing him. Her eyes opened, and he watched her response as his thumb slid over the sensitive button again and again.

"Sweet Jesus," she said on a groan. Rory grinned wickedly and kissed the underside of one breast, before making a pathway down her flat belly to the soft, downy curls that guarded her most treasured prize.

He breathed deeply of her scent and then tasted her.

Shannon gripped his head, her nails digging into his scalp as he licked her again, from back passage to the tight bundle of nerves at the top of her sex.

Delicious tremors rushed through her entire body as he continued to pleasure her with his tongue, each lick bringing her closer and closer to a wonderful pinnacle that she desperately reached for.

He gripped her buttocks with his large hands and brought her sex to his face. His tongue slid inside her hot core before lifting her clit, flicking relentlessly, and then alternately sucking slowly.

Her hands moved from his hair to the bedding, her fingers fisting the blankets at her sides as he continued his passionate onslaught.

Rory watched her under lowered lids as he pleasured her. He could see the shock and surprise in her eyes as she reached for orgasm. Her ice-blue eyes locked with his as he slid his finger into her again, while licking her tiny pearl. It was all that was needed to push her over the edge.

Shannon cried out as she shot to the heavens like an arrow and then shattered. A wonderful throbbing rocked her entire lower body, crashing over her like a wave against the sands.

Rory's cock was rock hard against her leg, and she felt him shift and move, settling once again between her widely spread thighs.

Although she'd just experienced pleasure the likes of which she'd only dreamed, she knew there was more bliss ahead. How she craved to have his long shaft buried deep inside her.

She just had to ignore the warning bells ringing in her head. He kissed her passionately, and she reared back a moment when she tasted herself on his lips.

But Rory would have none of it. He kissed her again, his tongue like velvet against her own. Her fingers wove into his hair, and she lifted her hips, desperate to finish what they had started.

Somewhere in the outer reaches of her mind, she heard a click, and it took her a moment to realize that someone had opened the chamber door and then as quickly had closed it.

Oh dear God. Who had it been?

9

All the excitement Shannon had been experiencing faded in the face of discovery.

Rory kissed her again, but she pulled away. "Someone just opened the door. Did you not hear it?"

"No," he said, looking not at all disturbed or worried by the news. "It was probably just a servant."

Just a servant? *She* was "just a servant."

"I must go before whoever saw us alerts Edward and I lose my job."

"You will not lose your job, Shannon," he said, brushing her hair back from her face.

But no reassurance could possibly set her mind at ease. She pushed him away and scrambled off the bed. Her chemise had been tossed beside the bed, and she trembled as she reached for it.

Rory's cock was like marble against his belly, and seeing Shannon's naked body was not helping. She had gained weight in the past month, and though still slender, he liked how her hips had a slight curve to them. Her legs were long and he could already envision them wrapped around his waist. Pale curls covered her sex, and her belly was flat, her waist small, and her breasts a perfect handful each, tipped by pale pink nipples that were still in tight little buds.

She lifted the chemise, slid it over her lithe body, and then looked at him. "My wrap," she said. He eased the garment from beneath him without taking his eyes off her.

She took it from him, thrust her arms into the sleeves, and tied the belt. "I shall return with some water for you. You must drink something besides liquor."

Seeing she was quite over the amorous mood, he fell back onto the mattress with a frustrated sigh. "I don't want water. I want you."

She ached to tell him that she wanted him, too, but she kept silent and left the room.

"Shannon," Lord Graston said, looking genuinely surprised to see her leaving his brother's room in the dead of night. Apparently her employer hadn't been the one to open the door minutes before.

"Lord Graston, I did not expect you home so soon."

"When I received the news, I left Harlech as soon as I could."

"And Lady Rochester, is she here?"

"No, she is making her way back with Marilyn, but at a more sensible pace, and by carriage, not horseback."

That much was a relief. She feared the other woman would take one look at her and know what had transpired. Lady Graston had such a way of reading a person. "Well, I shall not keep you, then, my lord. I know you must be anxious to see Lord Ambrose."

He nodded, his hand on the doorknob. "Edward told me that you have been watching after my brother quite diligently. Thank you for that."

"Of course," she replied, anxious to be away, in her room where she could once again think straight.

Victor opened the door and Rory glanced at them. His lips spread into a wide smile seeing his brother, and Shannon walked away, her mind returning to the heated moments in the bed-chamber.

Her nipples were still sensitive from where Rory had touched and kissed them, and she still felt an ache between her thighs.

Heated memories rushed through her, and she hid a smile as she entered the room to her small chamber. She stopped short seeing Zachary sitting in the chair beside the window, his expression one of concern.

She swallowed hard. "Zachary, what are you doing?"

He ran a hand down his face. "The question is: What are *ye* doing, Shannon?"

Her heart lurched. "What do you mean?"

"Did you not hear the door open, or were ye so enraptured by that rakehell that you did not hear me?"

Heat rushed to her cheeks and she shifted on her feet. What could she possibly say to defend herself? He had caught her red-handed.

"I had been roused to receive Lord Graston and I came to wake you, because I did not know if Lady Graston was with him, and I thought she would want you to assist her, but you were gone, and I was concerned. I see that I had every reason to be."

How utterly humiliating. She had been naked beneath Rory, and there was no misinterpreting what he had seen.

If there was one saving grace about the entire situation, it was that she could trust her brother not to say anything. No one else would keep their mouth closed.

"Shannon, do not be foolish. You know the man's reputation. He is dangerous, and I know for certain he came from a night with Lady Anna. Johnny could not quit speaking of it after he brought him home."

There was a part of her that wanted to know what the other man had said about Rory and Anna, but Shannon realized the two had a history together. Anna was a lady, Rory's peer, while she was a servant. A plaything and nothing more.

"Perhaps ye should ask to return to your other duties?" He stood and crossed his arms over his chest. "Shannon, the worst mistake ye could make is giving yourself to him."

He was right. She did not need to give up her maidenhead to a scoundrel. It would be a huge, irreversible mistake. "I shall . . . first thing tomorrow."

Taking a deep breath, he released it and shook his head. "Get some rest, and be sure to speak with Edward in the morning. Lord Ambrose is obviously well enough that he does not require constant care."

Rory was happy to see his brother. He just wished Victor's timing had been better.

Like half an hour later.

The bed dipped beneath Victor's weight as he sat down beside him. He could not recall the last time he had seen such a concerned expression on his sibling's face.

Victor leaned close and eased the bandage back. Seeing the wound, he frowned. "Bloody hell, Rory, you nearly got yourself killed this time."

Touched by his concern, and yet oddly annoyed at his paternal tone, Rory shrugged. "I think you forget that I got off lightly compared to Lord Cordland."

"Indeed, I heard," he murmured, fixing the bandage. "I'm just glad you're okay. My heart sank to my stomach when I heard the news you'd been injured. Poor Lillith, she wanted to come with me on horseback, but I insisted she travel by carriage."

He had gotten here in an incredible amount of time. "You traveled through the night?"

"I haven't slept for two days. Well, aside from a half an hour nap, but that was while I was waiting for a change of horse."

"I'm touched, Vic. Honestly, I didn't expect you for days."

"You'd do the same for me, and well you know it."

It was true. He'd move heaven and earth to be by his brother's side in a time of need. "I have no idea if they've been able to locate Sinjin and Katelyn, but I understand Mother and Father have been alerted."

"This is the last thing Mother needs."

"Yes, well, then let this be the last duel, Rory. Honestly, you need to put this life behind you. The surgeon said that had the bullet hit one inch to the left, you could have died."

"Then I am lucky for that inch. Trust me, brother, it is nothing more than a flesh wound, really."

"Flesh wound, my ass. And what is this about going out this evening? How very foolish."

Apparently Edward could not keep his mouth shut.

Victor pressed a hand to Rory's forehead. "You're perspiring and are exceedingly pale. Should I call for the physician?"

"Stop it," Rory said, pushing his brother's hand away. "You are hovering already."

The intensity left his brother's eyes and he laughed under his breath. "I suppose I am."

"Go to bed. I am tired, and I am sure you are as well."

"Before I leave you, I want you to consider staying here. Living here with us. Lily and I talked about it on the way to Wales. Now that this has happened, she will be even more adamant you stay."

"Sinjin said I could stay at the townhouse."

"It is being renovated." Victor folded his hands in his lap. "Plus, you asked to come here in your darkest hour, which means you want to be here ... with me. And Lord knows someone needs to keep their eye on you ... and Sinjin has a baby on the way."

He looked awfully full of himself, but Rory had to admit that he liked the idea of moving in with Victor, especially with a certain beautiful blonde underfoot. Rory sat up straighter. "If you insist, then, yes, I shall stay."

Victor grinned wholeheartedly. "Good, but there is one condition of staying with me."

"And what would that be?"

"You must keep your hands off the servants. Lily insists."

Damnation.

"Shannon is excellent help and a complete innocent, or I am hoping she is still innocent."

"Of course she is still innocent. She has proven herself to be a stellar nurse in my time of crisis."

"Do not touch her, Rory. You will only break her heart, and Lillith would be most displeased. She has grown quite attached to the girl."

Rory ran a hand through his hair. "What do you know of her?"

"Not a lot. I believe Lillith said she and her brother come from Scotland." He scrubbed a hand over the shadow of a beard that covered his jaw. "Come to think of it, she mentioned that there was a bit of a discrepancy on where exactly. When asked where in Scotland they hailed from, the boy said Edinburgh, while the girl said Inverness."

"Did Lillith not think that was odd?"

"She didn't push them for an answer, and honestly, they've been such excellent help that she didn't want to frighten them away with too many questions. Let's face it, everyone has secrets."

Indeed, he was right. Not wanting to get Shannon or her brother into trouble, he nodded. "Go to bed. You look horrible."

"Says the man who took a bullet to the shoulder," Victor said, mussing Rory's hair. "I can take a hint. I shall leave you alone for the night." He leaned down and placed a kiss on the top of Rory's head. "I love you, Rory. I hope you know that."

Rory smiled, surprised by the unexpected display of affection. "Of course, I do. I love you, too, Vic."

Clinton was nervous as he followed the butler into the parlor of the fashionable townhouse in the Mayfair District.

Lady Anna had invited him here, and knowing she was a link to get to Lord and Lady Graston by way of Lord Ambrose, he would do whatever he needed to.

Hopefully Rory would be here tonight.

"Mr. O'Connor, it's good to see you again," Thomas said, a welcoming smile on his face.

"Thank ye for having me, Mr. Lehman."

"Can I interest ye in a brandy?"

"Certainly."

It was then Clinton noticed Anna, sitting in the far corner of the room.

"Lady Anna," he said in greeting, and she smiled.

"Is Lord Ambrose not coming?" he inquired.

"You just missed him, I'm afraid," she murmured. "He was not feeling well."

He was disappointed when he realized it would be just the three of them, but he was a patient man.

Thomas walked across the room and poured a drink. The servant who had met them at the door had disappeared and the house fell quiet, except for the ticking of the second hand on the clock above the mantel.

"I have a little treat," Thomas said, handing Clinton the glass of brandy. He motioned to Anna, who went to the side cupboard. Making herself at home, she pulled out a pipe and a little box.

Next, she kicked off her shoes and sat on the settee, bringing her knees up beneath her.

Intrigued, Clinton stepped farther into the room.

Thomas blew out a few of the candelabras so that only a few candles lit the space. He then joined Anna on the settee and motioned for Clinton to come over. Soon the room was pungent with the sweet scent of opium.

Never before had he tried the drug, and he hesitated, not wanting to lose control in any way. Yet he didn't want to destroy his chances at building a friendship that would get him what he wanted.

Anna pulled a small white bead out of the box and set it in the bowl of the pipe. Apparently, she was no stranger to the drug. She brought the pipe to her lips, leaned forward, over the oil lamp, and slowly began to inhale the smoke into her lungs.

She closed her eyes, her lips curving into a smile as she handed the pipe to Clinton.

Almost instantly her shoulders relaxed. How bad could it be? he thought to himself, taking the pipe into his hand and bringing it to his lips. Anna sat back on the settee, a dreamy look in her eyes. Thomas assisted him with the lamp and Clinton inhaled, the smoke filling his lungs.

Within seconds he could feel the drug's effect as warmth spread throughout his limbs. He felt fingers brush against his hand. The pipe was removed from his relaxed fingers by Thomas, who winked at him.

"Lovely, isn't it?"

"Mmmm," he replied, already understanding the appeal of the drug, and why so many had sampled its healing ways. He closed his eyes, and when he next opened them, he saw Thomas and Anna kissing on the settee, the man's hand covering a small breast. Her gown had been loosened and bunched about her waist. The other man lowered his head and kissed her rose-hued nipples, first one, then the other.

Clinton kept his gaze lowered but could not ignore the throbbing in his groin.

Anna unbuttoned Thomas's trousers, her hand finding his cock, fisting it. The man smiled, and when she pushed him onto his back, he let out a little laugh and then a moan as she took him into her mouth.

His mouth was as dry as cotton, and he yearned to reach for the whiskey, but he didn't dare move. His cock was now hard against his belly, and he was grateful for the dark room so that his companions could not see his excitement.

Anna aggressively sucked and laved the other man's cock. Clinton let his gaze wander over Thomas's solid frame, the wide chest, the chiseled abdomen, the thick cock.

Thomas's hand stilled her movements and she looked up at him with a knowing smile.

Clinton's manhood quivered against his leg.

Anna straddled Thomas, and he rested his hands on her hips, easing her down on his length.

Clinton had last made love to a prostitute in a seedy Dublin club, and that was nearly two months ago.

Watching the duo was agonizing. He barely shifted and the slight movement made him grit his teeth as the material tightened on his bulge.

Lady Anna's firm breasts bounced as she rode her lover, her back arching.

She was exquisite.

He kept his gaze averted as Anna rode Thomas to completion, their cries rising to the high ceiling.

Anna fell on top of Thomas, and his arms came around her. Clinton's body was on fire; he got up, intent to find a dark corner and release the burn.

"Where are you going?" Thomas asked, looking over at him.

Clinton shook his head. "I just need some air."

He nodded and eased Anna up. The lady looked at Clinton with a coy smile, and he wondered if the two hadn't been aware of their audience all along.

"Don't be long. I have more opium," Thomas said, his gaze shifting down Clinton's body.

He left the room, trying to make sense through the haze that filled his mind. Perhaps he should leave before he did something he would regret.

But then again, he hadn't asked a single question about Lord Graston. He needed to get into the manor where his young cousins lived, and the only way he could get close was through the two individuals here, which meant he had to stay.

Thought of his cousins was enough to cool his heated blood, and after smoking a cigar, he returned to the parlor that smelled of sex and opium.

"Would you like another?" Thomas asked, bringing the pipe to his lips and inhaling.

"I think I've had enough, but I will have another whiskey."

Anna wore just a chemise, her nipples erect against the silk and she lounged on the settee, watching Thomas. He wondered if this was a common pastime of the two. As though reading his thoughts, she glanced over at him, a brow lifting high.

"Have you been to Lord Graston's home?" Clinton asked, feeling bold and confident.

"Yes, I have," Anna said, toying with a blond curl. "And I shall be attending their little soiree next week," Anna said nonchalantly. "Actually, it's more of a dinner party."

"I certainly won't be invited," Thomas replied with a scowl.

"Why not?" Clinton asked.

"Lord Graston and his eldest brother, Lord Mawbry, do not particularly care for Thomas here," Anna said, brushing her hand over Thomas's bicep.

"Why is that?"

"They are threatened by me," Thomas said with a roguish smile. "Or, rather, they are afraid of me seducing their wives away from them."

Anna snorted. "Those women are hopelessly in love with their husbands, and there is not a chance in hell that you, or any other man, would ever have a chance. Plus, neither Rory nor Victor has trouble with self-confidence . . . but if one of them doesn't like you for whatever the reason, the other will follow suit. They are as thick as thieves that way. Extremely loyal to each other."

Thomas shrugged. "One never knows. They might warm to me one day . . . like Lady Graston has."

Rolling her eyes, Anna went up onto her elbow and looked at Clinton. "You should come with me to the party, Clinton. I'm allowed to bring a guest, and you are more adventurous than most of my friends, present company excluded, of course," she said, winking at Thomas.

"Yes, you should go, Clinton," Thomas urged. "Lady Graston is a dear, and I understand her parties are incredible. Just be sure to report back to me."

Clinton had to bite his lip to keep from grinning like a fool. He had done it! He had found a way into the proverbial lion's den.

10

Shannon tried not to make eye contact, but it was nearly impossible. Now that Rory was residing at the manor permanently, she could not avoid him, nor could she stop thinking about him. He had been moved to the west wing, and since her duties focused around the kitchen and meals, she saw him only during meals.

Every time she opened the double doors to the dining room, her heart gave a lurch. She could not forget the feel of his hands on her body, the way he had tasted her most private place, or the way she had wanted him buried deep inside her.

Had they not been interrupted by her brother opening the chamber door, then she would have given up her maidenhead.

But everything happened for a reason, as her mother had always said, and in this case, she knew she should be happy that she had been saved from making a grave mistake. After all, giving her virginity to a rakehell would be a devastating and irreparable event.

And yet her heart nearly fluttered out of her chest when she saw him.

Dressed casually in a cream linen shirt and soft brown trousers, Rory sat back in his chair. He did not make eye contact with her, but she could sense his gaze on her every once in a while when she was serving.

When she passed Johnny in the kitchen doorway, the servant had grinned at her, and she smiled in return.

Rory shifted in his seat, and when she looked at him, his jaw was clenched tight.

Was he jealous?

Carrying a small silver tray in her hands without spilling anything, she approached him, offering a variety of cold meats. She stood close, her skirts brushing his hip. She felt his hand touch her leg, just the slightest pressure, but it was enough to set her blood on fire.

He pointed to a piece of duck. With a trembling hand, she pierced the meat with the serving fork and slid it onto his plate.

Her heart began to pound, and she could feel heat rush up her neck as he stared at her. For the next hour she continued to serve and was relieved when Cook said that she could be excused for the night. Tomorrow would be an eventful day. Lady Graston and her niece Marilyn were expected to arrive.

Exhausted from lack of sleep the night before, she went straight to her room, closed the door, and removed the uniform she was truly beginning to detest. She knew she should be grateful for her circumstances, but it was difficult when she yearned for the life she had once had. She wanted to wear pretty dresses and jewels, and dine with family and friends, not spend the rest of her days in servitude.

Removing the pins from her hair, she ran her fingers through the tresses, mourning for all she had lost. For so long she had not allowed herself to give in to her grief, to even think about all that had been *ripped* away from her and Zachary, but now she could not help the sadness and bitterness that consumed her.

Tears burned her eyes as she realized that she would never know that kind of security again, or that kind of unconditional love. The love of a mother and father for their child.

The door opened. "Zachary, I'll talk with ye tomorrow. I'm in no mood for company tonight."

The steps came closer and she turned.

It wasn't Zachary. It was Rory, and he looked extremely concerned. "What's wrong, Shannon? What has happened?"

Seeing him in her small, modest chamber was too much. He had consumed her every waking thought, and it scared her. Scared her that the thought of leaving the manor and her position would remove her from him. Scared that one day he would marry a woman of his same station and he would leave here, and she would be forgotten.

"Nothing," she said, letting the tears fall. "And everything."

He pulled her down on the bed and cupped her face with his strong hands. "Tell me, Shannon. What has happened to distress you so?"

His touch was heaven. Everything about him consumed her—his powerful body, the musky scent that completely enveloped her, drawing her into his web.

He brushed her tears away with his thumbs and kissed her gently.

"What is wrong, Shannon? You can tell me."

Unable to explain herself, she went into his arms and pressed her cheek against his chest, holding so tight she did not want to let go. He kissed her forehead, and she lifted her face to his. His lips were gentle, so soft, and yet firm. Her arms wrapped around his strong shoulders, and she pressed her breasts against his wide chest.

She wanted only to feel, to not think about all that she had lost, but to know what it felt like to be desired. To experience raw passion.

She opened her mouth to him and groaned when his tongue slid against hers, like the softest velvet. His long hair tickled her hand, and she caressed a strand between thumb and forefinger.

He eased her back upon the cot; she opened her eyes. He stared at her, gauging her reaction. "Shannon, are you sure?"

She nodded, never so positive of anything.

They kissed for long minutes, and she felt the familiar stirring in her belly, the intense need that coursed through her veins.

His hands moved to her breasts, his long fingers playing with the rigid peaks. Warmth flooded the flesh between her thighs, and she reached for his shirt, yanked it out of his trousers, needing desperately to feel the hot, olive skin beneath.

Rory's heart was a roar in his ears. He had not expected to come to her room in order to make love to her. He had missed her, and he'd been yearning for the sight of her. Seeing her at dinner was not near enough.

Tonight he could sense something was amiss with her just by her demeanor.

"Shannon," he said again, wanting her to tell him to stop now if she was in any way uncertain.

In answer she reached for the buttons of his trousers. Within seconds she had his cock in hand, her hand wrapping around his length.

He was so hard. He had to still her hand to keep from coming. Glancing at the small cot and realizing that another servant slept on either side of the thin walls, he lifted her in his arms, ready to take her to his chamber, but she shook her head. "I can't wait. I want you now."

She pulled him down on top of her, and he lifted her skirts. She was already so hot, so wet, and when she guided him to her entrance, he pushed all his misgivings aside and slid slowly inside her heat, easing past the thin membrane of skin that proved he was the first.

Shannon winced against the pain and bit down on her lip as he slid slowly inside, inch by inch, until he was fully inside her.

A primal moan vibrated in his chest. He stared down at her, his eyes so intense as he began to move.

With each slow thrust of his lower body, the pain began to ebb and a tightening sensation started deep inside. Her gaze shifted to his lovely full lips, and he lowered his head and kissed her.

Rory kept his need in check, a difficult task with her hot sheath clamped around him. She started to move with him, arching her hips, and he moaned again, pleased by her response.

Her nails grazed his shoulders, and the kiss deepened. He could tell she was close to climax, could feel the pounding of her heart against his own.

Shannon felt a similar sensation to when he had kissed her in her most intimate place, but this was stronger, more powerful, and as he ground his hips snug against her sensitive button, she cried out.

He made a pleased sound and slowed his pace, pulling away just enough to look down at her. He stared at her, and she was shocked by the intensity in his eyes. There was such a heaviness about his lids, the brilliant blue irises were dark, and she realized what she was seeing was desire.

Did he see the same thing when he looked at her? Was her desire obvious?

Watching Shannon climax had been exhilarating and had made his need even greater.

Rory lowered his head and kissed her breast, his mouth covering her nipple. He barely moved his lower body, and she found herself lifting her hips, wanting his entire length inside her. *Needing* him buried deep inside her.

His teeth grazed the sensitive peak, before sucking and laving the other. Her hands moved from his broad shoulders, down his strong back, to the high, firm globes of his buttocks.

Apparently he liked what she was doing, because he smiled, his lips finding hers once more, his strokes faster and more fluid by the second.

Her stomach tightened as she came again, and he followed fast behind, their moans mingling.

Rory woke to find Marilyn sitting in a chair beside his bed, reading a book.

"Marilyn, you have returned."

She glanced up from her reading. "We came as quickly as we could. Ah, I didn't wake you, did I?" she asked, looking sheepish.

He shook his head. He had only just returned to his bed a few hours ago, after an incredible night of making love to Shannon.

It had been the single sweetest encounter of his life, and already he ached to see her again.

"How are you feeling?"

"Quite well, actually."

"You are fortunate you are young and fit. I cannot believe how fast you've recovered."

"I am," he agreed. He sat up against the headboard, wondering how to broach a most uncomfortable subject. "I am glad you have come to visit. I had a visitor the other night who was asking about you."

She sat up straighter. "Oh, and who would that be?"

"Lady Anna."

Marilyn dropped her gaze to the floor between them. "I need not ask what she wanted."

"She wishes to talk to you again."

"There is nothing to say."

"I told her as much, and I told her you were happy with your baron."

Marilyn sighed heavily. "She does not care, Rory. Indeed, I believe she enjoys making everyone around her uncomfortable."

Their friend did have a tendency of rubbing people the wrong way and took a perverse satisfaction in doing so.

"I hope you don't mind, but I've invited her to the soiree this next week."

"Rory!"

"She is my friend, Marilyn," he said, uncomfortable with the fact she was agitated with him.

"And I am now your family. I would think your loyalty would fall to me."

Now he felt guilty. "I can tell her not to come."

"No, we are all adults. I just do not want her making a scene."

"She would not make a scene," he said, making a promise to himself to keep a tight rein on Anna the night of the soiree. "So . . . how was your trip?"

Marilyn instantly relaxed. "Wonderful. Wales is so beautiful. I especially loved Harlech Castle. One can imagine what life must have been like during the times of Llewellyn the Great."

"I would like to see it for myself one day."

There was a slight rap at his door, and his heart actually gave a leap. He hoped it was Shannon, but it wasn't. It was Edward.

"My Lord, I wanted to inform you that your mother has arrived."

"Oh dear God," he said, and Marilyn laughed aloud and promptly clamped a hand over her mouth.

"Thank you, Edward."

Edward nodded and closed the door.

"I'm sorry," Marilyn said, looking not at all apologetic.

All he wanted was time alone with Shannon, but he could tell that would be a luxury long in coming, especially with his mother staying on.

"Can I get you anything?"

"A gun, perhaps?" he said.

"Rory," she said with a smile. "I think you have had enough experience with guns to last you a lifetime."

"I would ask for a whiskey, but Mother would not approve." He released a breath. "Do me a favor. Tell her that I am taking a bath, and that I shall meet her downstairs in the dining room with the others for breakfast."

"Very well. I will see you soon."

11

"My dearest boy," Betsy said, her arms flung wide open when Rory walked into the dining room. "How happy I am to see you."

"Thank you, Mother," Rory replied, locked in a rose-scented bear hug.

"How is Father?"

"Well, and he sends his love," she said, dropping her gaze to his cravat.

He knew his father was very ill and had seen his frail health for himself.

"I am sorry that you had to leave him."

"You are my son. And when my son needs me, I shall go. Your father would be here himself if he could be."

She pulled an imaginary string off his jacket. "I do so worry about you. You know, if you married, then the gossipmongers would have nothing more to talk about."

"The duel was not my idea, Mother. He called me out."

"With good reason, I understand," she said, biting her lip as though she had said far too much. "Come, sit down and get off your feet."

Rory glanced at his brother, hoping in some way that he would jump in, but Victor seemed preoccupied, staring straight ahead. It always did take a while for his brother to wake up in the morning.

Lillith entered the room, a vision in an emerald green day dress, and seeing Rory, she clapped her hands together. "Brother, you are a sight for sore eyes."

"Lillith," Rory said fondly, embracing her.

A servant walked in and Rory glanced toward the door, his heart missing a beat. It was Candice.

He released a disappointed breath.

"Lillith, you shall have to help me talk Rory into marrying," Betsy said, mischievous smile in place.

Lillith grinned widely. "But he must find the right woman, and as you should know from your other sons' recent marriages, finding a spouse on one's own has merit."

"A little help never hurt," his mother said in a way that meant he could count on her interference.

"And I appreciate your efforts, Mother, but I can manage."

"Hell will freeze first," Betsy muttered beneath her breath.

Before he could ask specifically what she meant, the door to the kitchen opened and Shannon appeared. His pulse skittered with excitement.

She was dressed in a blue gown with a floral print that brought out the color of her eyes. He was so accustomed to seeing her in her gray uniform, it was almost startling to see her otherwise. Her pale blond hair was down around her shoulders and he was reminded of last night, of burying his nose in her curls, of taking her beneath him.

He had never before been with a virgin, and he was unprepared for the feelings racing through him. He felt possessive and protective all at once. Just the thought of her being with another man made him furious.

"Rory!"

His mother snapped her fingers and he glanced at her. "Yes?"

She was frowning at him, her brow lifted high as she glanced at Shannon and then back at him.

"I asked if you were feeling well enough to attend the soiree your brother and Lillith are throwing next week."

"Of course. I feel as strong as ever."

"Do not let him fool you, Mother," Victor said, sounding remarkably like their father. "He needs his rest."

He glared at Victor, who ruffled Rory's hair as he walked past.

Shannon walked toward Lillith and whispered in her ear. Lillith nodded, then stood. "Marilyn and I are heading into London. Is there anything that you need?"

"Nothing but your safe return, my dear," Victor said.

Rory refrained from rolling his eyes. What had happened to his brother?

"Is Shannon going with you?" Rory asked, now understanding why she was dressed the way she was.

Shannon's eyes widened a little and her cheeks turned bright pink.

"Why, yes, she is. Why do you ask?" Lillith asked, her gaze darting to Shannon, who shifted on her feet.

His mother kicked him beneath the table and he shook his head. "I just noticed she was out of uniform. That is all."

"Oh, yes, I do not see a need for her to wear her uniform today," Lily remarked, giving him a look that said to be careful. "Well, we should get going."

Shannon nodded, and looked ready to bolt for the door.

Rory willed her to glance his way, but she did not spare him a glance.

Lillith hesitated at the door. "I am so pleased to have you in my home, Lady Rochester. I look forward to visiting with you tonight." She glanced at her niece. "Marilyn, are you coming?"

Marilyn grabbed her untouched scone, wrapped it in a napkin, and followed Lillith out the door.

Rory was desperate to follow her, to pull Shannon into his arms and tell her how he had dreamt of her . . . that he yearned to be with her again.

"I shall see them to the carriage," Victor said, disappearing before Rory could give him the "save me from Mother" look.

The door shut behind them, and Rory had no choice but to make eye contact with his mother.

"Rory, do not be foolish."

He frowned. "What are you talking about, Mother?"

"You know bloody well what I'm talking about. You are looking at that servant girl like she is a sweet and you'd like to gobble her up."

He shifted in the chair. "I think she is attractive."

"Tell me she is not the reason you decided to move in with your brother?"

Doing his best to school his features, he looked her straight in the eye. "You gave the London townhouse to Sinjin, Mother, and he is knee-deep in renovations. Where else would you want me to stay?"

"I am not discouraging you from staying with Victor. He does dote on you, so I understand why you would wish to stay, but I also worry if there is not another reason that you are here."

"Mother, you need not con—"

"Your father and I still expect you to marry, my dear."

Good God, is marriage all the woman ever thought about?

He slouched in the chair, knowing full well it would irritate the hell out of her. He could see her mentally counting to ten as her jaw clenched tight.

She sighed heavily and closed her eyes, for all of four seconds. "Well, I would still like to introduce you to Lady Kinkade. She is a lovely woman. About your age and widowed for several years now, I believe. I have invited her to your brother and sister-in-law's soiree."

Of course she had.

He saw the wheels in her mind turning, and it made him nervous.

"Please do not push your friends and acquaintances on me, Mother."

Where the hell was Victor? Certainly it didn't take him this long to say good-bye to his wife? He was clearly stalling.

"You will be kind to Lady Kinkade, Rory."

"Of course I shall." He stood, anxious to be away from her company. Kissing her on the cheek, she smiled and sat back in her seat.

He rushed toward the door.

"Where are you going?" Betsy inquired.

"I need fresh air." Feeling guilty for leaving her alone, he asked, "Would you like to join me?"

"No, I'm exhausted from my journey. I can never sleep in the carriage. I will return to my chamber and take a long nap before dinner. Thank you for asking me."

"Of course," he replied, relieved and wishing Shannon had stayed.

Shannon had absolutely no desire to go shopping with Lillith, but she was in no position to argue, especially since her mistress was adamant she attend to her and Marilyn. Even more shocking, she had told her to change out of her uniform and into a dress.

So Shannon had done just that. She had hoped to leave the house before seeing Rory but had not been so fortunate. When Lillith had told her to come to the dining room when she was ready, Shannon had stalled for time, hoping that the household would be finished with breakfast and off to their own devices. Unfortunately, everyone, including Lady Rochester, had been there, and she had not been happy by Rory's attention to Shannon at all.

Hopefully word was not circulating around the manor about a liaison between herself and Rory. When she had awoken this morning, with blood stains on the white sheets and a soreness between her thighs, she knew that she'd made a grave error. She had let her heart lead her to make a decision that could have serious consequences. What if she carried Rory's child? If she thought her life a mess now, a baby would only complicate matters. She knew well enough what happened to pregnant servants and mistresses.

Stupid, stupid, stupid.

"I am so looking forward to spending some time alone with you, Shannon. I confess I missed your companionship while we were in Wales," Lillith said, which surprised Shannon.

"She did miss you," Marilyn added, sitting back in the carriage seat.

"I missed you as well," Shannon said, smiling at Lillith. The smile slipped when she walked past the window. Her brother wore a beaver hat snug on his head, and his blond hair had been pulled back into a low queue. He had dark circles beneath his eyes, and when their eyes met, he looked concerned.

It was bad enough that either one of them was in town, but together they risked an even greater chance of being discovered.

Truth be told, she had fallen into a false sense of security since Lord Graston had returned, and she'd not given much thought to her cousin or the older gentleman she'd seen across the road from the manor the other day.

She could only hope their luck held out.

The ride into London was uneventful, and as the carriage pulled over and Zachary helped them out, Shannon reminded herself that the city was full of people and that it was akin to finding a needle in a haystack.

Unless, of course, they had been followed from the manor.

As she fell into step beside the other two women, she looked at the storefronts they passed by. Catching her reflection, she was startled, unused to seeing herself in plain clothes and her hair down. She looked like any other woman on the streets. Though her dress was plain, she did not feel like a servant.

"Aunt Lillith, let's go in there," Marilyn said, pointing toward a jewelry shop.

They browsed the store, looking into the glass cases, and Shannon was reminded of her mother's jewels that had been lost in the fire. Heirlooms that had been passed down from generation to generation.

"This would look just lovely on you," Lillith said, pointing to a beautiful cameo hanging from a gold necklace.

"Would you like to try it on, Shannon?"

"No, that is quite all right." She couldn't possibly afford the necklace on her wages, and honestly, when would she have the opportunity to wear it?

"Try it, Shannon," Marilyn urged, asking the store keeper to remove the beautiful piece.

"I shall buy it for you," Lillith said as a store assistant helped her. Shannon lifted her hair and waited while the clasp was secured.

"You are too generous, my lady."

"There is a mirror over here," the assistant said, motioning toward a nearby cheval mirror.

It was a beautiful cameo, and it looked lovely, but she did not want Lady Graston buying it for her. She had done so much for her and Zachary already.

"How lovely," Marilyn said, coming up from behind Shannon and smiling. "It suits you."

Shannon returned Marilyn's smile, until her gaze was drawn toward a man she saw in the mirror's reflection. Her heart sank to her stomach. It looked like Clinton.

"What is it?" Marilyn asked, glancing over her shoulder, to the street.

"Nothing. I just feel light-headed. Can we go?"

Marilyn nodded, but something in her expression made Shannon wonder if she truly believed her.

"Let us stop for tea," Lillith said, and the store attendant quickly removed the necklace.

Lillith and Marilyn stood on either side of Shannon, obviously concerned she would faint.

She felt badly for lying, but how could she tell them that a man was following her?

She scanned the street as they left the store, and she didn't see Clinton.

Were her eyes playing tricks on her?

They slipped into a nearby tea shop, and she breathed a sigh of relief when they sat at a table in a far corner.

Lillith handed Shannon a fan and she took it, grateful for the relief it would bring.

As the minutes passed and they were served tea, Marilyn and Lillith seemed to relax. Lady Graston stirred a teaspoon of sugar into her cup and looked at Shannon with a soft smile. "Shannon, my husband informs me that his brother has become smitten with you."

Shannon had the cup halfway to her mouth. She took a sip

of tea and managed to set it back down without spilling it everywhere.

"I am sure he is mistaken, my lady."

"I have seen the way he looks at you . . . and the way you look at him," she continued.

"He is a handsome man," Shannon murmured. "All the servants think so."

"Indeed," Marilyn said with a wink. "There is not a woman alive who would disagree. Now do not embarrass Shannon further, Aunt Lily."

"Forgive me, my dear, I did not mean to embarrass you."

A man stepped into the store and Shannon's stomach lurched. It was the man she had seen across the way from the manor the other day, she was certain of it. This could not be a coincidence, especially when she had just seen her cousin.

She looked outside, hoping to see Zachary.

The man passed a woman on the way out the door. He put a hand to the brim of his hat and nodded in greeting, before taking a seat nearby.

"Are you all right, my dear?" Lillith asked, reaching for Shannon's hand.

"I am fine, my lady. I'm just still a little dizzy."

"You must eat something," Marilyn said matter-of-factly.

Shannon's mind raced. What if she told Lady Graston the truth about her cousin? Would she offer protection? But what would Zachary say?

Marilyn immediately changed the subject to the upcoming soiree, and Shannon said very little. She could feel the man watching her, and she glanced toward the storefront, wondering if her cousin was lying in wait. Or worse still, what if Clinton had Zachary?

12

It didn't take Rory and Victor long to find the three women. They had stepped out of a tea shop and were now headed down the sidewalk.

Victor smiled and motioned for Rory to follow from across the street. Rory could see men of all ages staring at the beautiful trio, and he felt an odd combination of pride and jealousy.

When one man in particular stayed close, Rory nudged Victor. "Keep an eye on the older gentleman with the black top hat."

Victor frowned. "He's probably just admiring them."

"But when they linger, he lingers. Watch him."

Even more disconcerting was the fact that Shannon looked over her shoulder a time or two. Was she aware of the man?

"They are three beautiful women out on their own in the city. Perhaps he is merely admiring them," Victor said. "Or hoping for an opportunity to meet them."

The women stepped into a stationery store and the man's steps faltered. Victor no longer smiled. The man walked by the store, then stopped and leaned against the building.

"What the hell," Rory said, his eyes narrowing.

"Come on. Let's surprise them. That should take care of their admirer." Victor started across the road and Rory followed.

The man glanced at them, ran his fingers along the brim of his hat, and then started walking down the sidewalk.

"Very odd," Victor replied. "I swear he looked right at us."

"Indeed, he did. I have half a mind to run him down and beat him to a pulp."

"Forget him," Victor said, watching the man disappear in the crowd.

Rory had seen Shannon's face, had recognized the fear in her eyes, and wondered with a sickening feeling what she was hiding.

Shannon had wondered why the store had gone so quiet all of the sudden. The presence of two handsome men in a room full of mostly women had a way of drying up conversation.

Rory's blue eyes were on her and when he smiled, her heart gave a jolt.

"What a lovely surprise," Lillith said, embracing her husband.

"We came to see if you'd like to take a walk in the park," Victor said, looking pleased with himself.

"Are you sure you did not come to make sure I was not spending too much money?" Lily said teasingly.

Victor's eyes widened in mock innocence, and Marilyn laughed aloud.

As they exited the store, Shannon strained to see past the crowded streets toward the place where they had left Zachary and the carriage.

"Are you looking for someone?" Rory asked her, and she jumped.

"Yes, my brother."

"He is just over there, near the park," Lillith said, motioning toward the adjacent road, where sure enough, Zachary stood near the carriage. His hat was pulled down low over his eyes.

Shannon breathed a sigh of relief.

Marilyn quickened her step, and Shannon slowed her pace to keep in time with Rory.

As they walked along the park, Shannon became increasingly aware of Rory's appeal. There was not a single woman, or man for that matter, who did not stare at him. Next to him she felt insignificant, and even worse, when three young ladies walked by, they giggled, and she wondered if it was because of her plain dress. It had been the best she could afford on a servant's wages.

She felt Rory's hand on hers and every ounce of resistance evaporated. How she longed to lean into him and bury her face against his strong chest, to wrap herself in his embrace and tell him the truth about her past, and of her fears that her cousin had found them.

"I want to see you tonight," he whispered, making the blood in her veins positively burn.

"I shall try."

"Do more than try."

Marilyn looked back at them and smiled. Good Lord, she hadn't heard them, had she?

They walked around the pond in silence and she enjoyed being with him, listening to the birds in the trees, and watching people as they passed by, and yet she feared her cousin would appear.

Marilyn had stopped to talk to a friend, and Victor and Lillith were a good ways ahead.

Rory faltered and Shannon noticed how pale he had become. "You have done too much."

99

He didn't bother to deny it. "I should sit and catch my breath."

"Lord Graston," Shannon called out, and Victor glanced back at them, as did Lillith, whose smile quickly faded. Victor rushed toward them.

"I think the wound is bleeding," Rory said, placing a hand inside his waistcoat. His fingers came back bloodied.

Victor cursed under his breath.

Lillith looked alarmed. "What is it?"

"We need to go home."

"Certainly. I shall see if Marilyn can get a ride with her friends."

"It's nothing," Rory replied, but Shannon could tell he was putting on a brave face for them. Sweat beaded his brow.

"I can run ahead and have the carriage meet us at the park entrance," Shannon said, but Rory shook his head.

"No, I am fine. Just walk with me."

She nodded and slid her hand around his elbow. He was actually trembling now and she was afraid, or rather, *terrified* that he might have an infection and a fever.

They passed by a group in an open phaeton who had no doubt heard about the duel. Lord Cordland's name was said loudly, and a man mentioned scandal.

How very cruel people could be.

Shannon was relieved when she saw Zachary and the carriage. Victor motioned him over, and soon they were entering the carriage. Rory fell onto the velvet seat.

"Damn it," Victor said under his breath. "I should have never let him talk me into leaving the manor."

Zachary glanced at Shannon and quickly looked away as he closed the door and took his position on the perch above.

He looked concerned, but she had no way of knowing whether he was worried about her growing relationship with Rory, or if he'd seen Clinton or the gray-haired man.

"Should we call for the physician?" Lillith asked, concern in her eyes.

"Yes," Victor said, brushing a hand through his hair.

"No, I just need to rest," Rory said, leaning his head back against the carriage wall.

How she yearned to comfort him, to hold his hand, but she wouldn't in front of others.

It seemed an eternity before they pulled into the manor driveway. The carriage had barely rolled to a stop when Victor jumped down. "You are too weary. Let me carry you."

Rory lifted his brows. "Over my dead body."

Victor smiled for the first time since Rory had said he wasn't feeling well. "I can oblige you."

"Yes, I'm sure you could . . . and would. I am capable of walking."

Shannon followed them up the stairs and hesitated in the foyer, not sure what she should do.

Rory looked at her, and Lillith whispered, "Come, he needs you."

She nodded and rushed up the stairs after them. The west chamber that housed his new quarters was enormous, and light shone in from every window. She immediately closed the heavy blinds.

Victor helped Rory off with his shirt and told him to sit on the bed. Rory fell onto the mattress and barely moved as his brother set to removing his boots, stockings, and trousers.

Lillith had left the room the instant the shirt had come off, and Shannon made herself busy preparing the clean bandages.

"Why didn't you say something sooner?" Victor said, clearly exasperated.

"I didn't realize I would be so tired," Rory said.

"Your age is catching up with you."

"You are one to talk."

Shannon smiled at the banter and hoped that meant Rory was not too ill.

Edward brought in a bowl of warm water and some rags. "Can I get you anything else, my lord?"

"No, Edward," Victor replied. "That will be all. Thank you."

Shannon rolled up her sleeves, then went to the bed and peeled off the bandage.

Fluid had seeped out, and thankfully it was clear.

"It doesn't look infected."

"That's a relief," Victor said, leaning against the bedpost.

"He should have been in bed, and just did a little too much, too soon," she said reassuringly. "I have seen far worse."

Victor watched her closely. "See that he does not try to get up. He needs to rest; even if you must tie him to the bed."

Rory didn't open his eyes, but his lips curved.

"Quit hovering, Victor," he said a second later, and Victor laughed under his breath.

"I can take a hint. I'm obviously not wanted."

"Can you blame me?" Rory replied, glancing at Shannon.

"Not at all." Victor lingered for a few more minutes until Rory's irritated sighs sent him from the room.

"You are mean," Shannon murmured. "He only cares about you."

"He's being paranoid."

His muscled abdomen clenched beneath her fingers as he moved, and she marveled at the power in his over six-foot frame. He made her feel so impossibly female, and when his gaze settled on her, her stomach tightened.

He lifted his hand, his fingers toying with her nipple. The breath left her in a rush as the peak stabbed against her chemise and the bodice of her gown.

"Lock the door, Shannon." His voice was husky, and it sent a shiver of awareness through her.

"You are ill."

"No, I'm not. I'm merely tired . . . but not that tired."

She scowled at him, but did as he asked. "Don't be ridiculous. What if someone comes to check on you?"

"They won't."

"Your mother . . ."

"Victor promised me he would not rouse Mother from her nap."

He had no way of knowing that. "I will lose my job if we are caught."

"No, you won't. I wouldn't allow it." He patted the bed beside him, and she joined him. "Plus, Lillith adores you."

"You're exhausted." Her mind said no and yet her body said yes.

"I can sleep later."

He eased his upper body off the bed, his muscles moving beneath olive skin as he leaned toward her. His hands were at her back a moment later, then the gown was sagging around her waist. How had he worked so quickly? she wondered, as he tugged at the ribbon that held her chemise together. He bent slightly and kissed a naked breast, then the other.

She looked down at him, watched with fascination as his mouth closed around a nipple. Liquid fire roared through her veins, and a familiar throbbing pulsed between her thighs.

She realized she wanted him there, buried deep within her core, and the pulsing only intensified as he sucked, his teeth grazing the sensitive peaks.

He pushed the gown past her waist, and his hand was sliding in the slit of her drawers, where he cupped her woman's flesh. He slid one finger inside, followed by another. "You're so wet, Shannon," he said, sounding extremely pleased.

His cock tented his drawers, and she was amazed she could cause such a reaction without even touching him. He slid out of his undergarment and she took his cock in hand, sliding her hand up and down the thick length, her insides tightening as she anticipated what was to come.

He eased her on top of him, and cupping her bottom, he guided her onto his shaft. She licked her lips as his fingers wrapped around her hips and showed her the rhythm he liked.

She let her instincts take over and rode him, gripping his chest. Her body tightened with each stroke, her tiny pearl brushing against him, sending a shiver up her spine.

He cupped her breasts, his breath hot on a nipple before he laved it with his tongue, drawing it deep into his mouth.

She climaxed, her dew coating his cock.

With a moan, he flipped her, his strokes long and steady, the headboard hitting the wall with force.

Rory grit his teeth as he slid into her hot flesh.

When would he get enough of her? She was so beautiful, and he wanted to teach her everything about making love.

Her hands roved down his body, cupping his ass, her fingers pressing against him, coaxing him into a deeper stroke.

He slid one leg over his shoulder and she was reminded of when he'd taken Candice in a similar fashion. She could feel him so completely this way, the crown of his cock touching her womb.

His blue eyes were intense as he watched her reach for orgasm. She felt deliciously wicked as she glanced down at where their bodies were joined, his long shaft sliding in and out of her.

He waited until she came again. His fingertips pressed into her thigh as he pumped a few more times and came with a pleased groan.

13

Shannon knew she should get up. At any given moment, someone could open the chamber door and she would, in all likelihood, lose her position.

But she savored being in Rory's arms, of feeling the pounding of his heart against her chest, the touch of his fingers brushing along the length of her spine, the sensation of their naked bodies pressed together.

He made her forget completely about reason and made her forget that she must tell her brother about Clinton.

"Tell me about your life before coming to work for Lillith."

Her pulse skittered. She didn't want to lie to him, and yet, she couldn't break her promise to her brother to not tell anyone about their past.

"There isn't much to tell." She brushed a hand over his chiseled abdomen. The muscles clenched beneath her fingers, and tendrils of warmth worked through her belly.

Even after their fevered coupling, she still wanted him.

"I know you worked at Lady Dante's dress shop before

coming to work for Lady Graston. What other jobs have you held?"

"Same as what I do here."

"Was it a smaller household?"

She thought of her own household in Ireland. "Yes, but not by much."

"Have you and your brother always been close?"

"Yes."

"What will you do if one of you is to marry?"

Shannon glanced up at him. "We won't worry about that until the time comes."

One day it would be wonderful to reclaim what they had lost, but anymore she had so little faith that it would actually happen. She just wanted to live for the moment.

Not wanting to answer any more of his questions, she slid out of bed and slipped back into her drawers, chemise, and gown.

Rory leaned up on an elbow. "Where are you going?"

"You must rest, and you won't while I'm here."

"I don't want to rest. I want you to come back to bed."

He had no idea how tempted she was to do just that. "I can't. I'll lose my job." She knew she kept repeating herself, but it was a very real concern.

"No, you won't."

"You don't know that."

"My brother would never allow it. He cares too much about my happiness."

His happiness? Her eyes widened at that. Was he happy because of her? How long would he feel that way? she wondered.

"Plus, Lily adores you."

And she adored Lily. "I have to go, but I'll come back after dinner."

He reached out for her and squeezed her hand. "Give me a kiss."

She leaned down, and he pulled her on top of him. She kissed the curve of his ear and he let out a wonderful groan. "You little vixen."

"I have to go."

He sighed heavily. "Will you come to me tonight?"

"If I can."

"Please come."

As she slid off him and walked toward the door, she knew that she could never deny him.

Shannon woke to an insistent knock on her door. It was the middle of the night. She pulled on her wrap and answered the door. It was Edward.

"Lord Ambrose is very ill. The surgeon is on his way, and Lady Graston has asked for you to assist him when he arrives."

Her pulse skittered. "He did not seem unwell earlier. He slept all day, but I did not think—"

"His brother checked in on him and found him burning with fever."

She had gone to his room, but Rory had been sleeping so peacefully she hadn't awoken him. She'd touched his forehead, and finding it damp with perspiration, she opened the window a fraction to allow a cool breeze into the room. Hopefully she had not made matters worse.

"I shall get dressed and come to his chamber," she said, and he nodded.

Shannon hurried and dressed, then rushed toward Rory's chamber, her mind racing.

She entered Rory's quarters. Lord Graston stood beside his brother, and Lady Graston and Lady Rochester sat in nearby chairs. Lily smiled softly at Shannon, and as Shannon approached she was stunned at Rory's pallor.

"I shall check and see if the physician has come," Lord Graston said, walking out of the chamber, his wife's eyes following him.

Shannon reached out and touched Rory's forehead. He was burning up. "I left him four hours ago and he seemed fine."

"It is not your fault," Lady Rochester murmured. "He has been doing far too much for his own good. I fear we must be careful from here on out and not allow him to do anything but care for his shoulder. I swear I shall have him tied to the bed if need be."

The door flew open and Lord Graston and the physician walked in. Shannon stepped back, watching nervously as the man inspected the wound. "Have you been applying the ointment?" he asked her directly.

"Yes, sir," Shannon replied.

He frowned. "The wound is looking a little red along the edges. Although it is draining, I fear there is some pus."

Victor swore under his breath, and Lily put a hand on her husband's shoulder.

"I will leave some laudanum for you to administer to him. Make sure he takes it, for it is imperative he stay down and not move. He is very ill."

Shannon nodded and swallowed past the lump in her throat. She didn't know what she would do if something happened to Rory. She would feel responsible.

The room fell silent as the physician worked on the wound. Rory said something, but no one could make it out. When the physician finished, he left new dressings, another jar of ointment, and the laudanum with instructions.

The physician followed Lady Rochester out the door, and

Shannon wiped a rag across Rory's brow. "The sheets beneath him are wet. They should be changed."

"I'll get a fresh pair right away," Edward said, surprising Shannon. She had not even realized he had returned.

"Damn it, why did I take him into London? What was I thinking?" Victor said, running his hands through his hair and lacing his hands together behind his neck. "I should have known better. I was just so excited that he was well."

"Husband, stop blaming yourself," Lillith said, leaning over the bed and brushing a dark lock of hair over Rory's ear. "Your brother is a grown man and he would not want you fretting. I am sure he will be fine. He is young and strong, and far too stubborn to let a nasty thing like a bullet wound or fever get him down."

Victor's lips curved slightly and he nodded.

Edward arrived with clean linens.

"I shall help you pick him up, my lord," Edward said, handing Shannon the sheets.

It took them only a matter of minutes to have the sheets changed and Rory back on the bed. He had moaned a few times but made little movement.

"I think we should let him rest," Lillith said, standing.

"I will stay with him," Shannon said, but Victor shook his head.

"No, you go get your sleep, Shannon. I shall take tonight's shift. He will need you tomorrow."

She didn't want to leave Rory's side, but she couldn't very well tell her employer "no." "If you are certain, my lord."

"I am," he said, and all she could do was give Rory a last lingering look before walking out the door.

* * *

Thankfully, as the days went by, Rory improved. In fact, just seventy-two hours after that terrifying night his fever had come on, he sat up in bed and watched her as she stoked the fire.

"Come here," he said, his voice silky soft.

She knew that tone, knew what it meant. "You are too weak, my lord."

"No, I'm not."

"I have strict instructions from the physician that you are not to move. That is what got you into trouble in the first place, and I shall not have your brother coming down on me for endangering your life."

"I shall not tell. I promise."

Glancing over her shoulder, she smiled. She wanted to slip into bed with him. She burned to be taken by him, to feel his hands on her body, to feel his long shaft slipping inside her, stroking her until she cried out in ecstasy.

But they would both have to wait.

"I'll go crazy if I can't have you. Look at what you do to me."

His cock was rigid, swelling up toward his belly.

Her body responded in kind. The flesh between her thighs tingled.

"I want you."

He would not give up, she knew that, but she was also not going to risk doing anything that would endanger him.

Aware that the rest of the family was eating dinner, she felt safe knowing they would not be interrupted. She took his cock in hand and started stroking him, her fingers gripping him tight.

A pleased groan escaped his lips, and she lowered her head and licked the plum-sized crown. Her tongue slid over the velvety soft skin, swirling around, along the ridge, then over and down the length. He was too long to take completely into her mouth, but she did her best to relax her throat.

Rory's heart rate increased, and he cupped his hips as she took him deeper into her throat. His balls were so heavy, and he ached to pull her beneath him and bring her to climax over and over again.

His fingers slid into her hair, and his breathing grew more ragged the closer he came to orgasm. He was close. She could tell by the way he put his hand on her shoulder, stilling her movements. She would stop for a moment, her mouth hovering above his cock, and then relax, and she would slowly, tentatively lick him.

He touched her breast, his fingers toying with a nipple through her uniform. The peak stabbed against the fabric, and she felt a wave of desire ripple through her straight to her molten core.

She quickened her pace, sucking, laving until he was pumping against her, his breathing harsh.

"Shannon," he said on a moan, and a second later hot semen shot into the back of her throat.

Rory released a long groan and slid his arm around her waist, pulling her close.

"Your shoulder," she said, concern marring her brow.

"Will be fine. For now I just want to hold you."

Rory was stunned by her actions. He had not expected her to pleasure him the way she had. She was a quick study, that was for certain, and he wondered what other surprises were in store for him.

"You need to rest, my lord."

She kissed his forehead, and his hand cupped her face. "You please me in every way, do you know that?"

And his words pleased her.

"Do I?"

"More than you will ever know."

She hoped he was not just saying as much to pacify her, as

men were known to do. Giving him the benefit of the doubt, she smiled softly and pulled away. "I must get going. I promised Lady Graston I would help her with her hair this evening."

"Does Lily not have a lady's maid?"

"She does, but tonight is the servant's night off."

He gave an exaggerated sigh. "Ah, I see."

"I shall check on you later this evening."

"What time?" he asked, looking anxiously at the clock.

"Before I retire. Ten o'clock, perhaps?" she said, opening the door.

"I'll be waiting."

Exhausted from a long day, Shannon walked into Rory's chamber and smiled seeing Victor reading to him.

"I have come to check the dressing," she said, approaching Rory. As always when she was around him, her heart began to pound hard in her chest, and she noted the way he watched her so intently. Was their attraction obvious to Victor, who had stopped reading?

"You need not stop reading on my account, Lord Graston," Shannon said. "I will not be long."

"He was just leaving," Rory said, flashing his brother a smile.

Victor snapped the book closed. "I know when I am not wanted," he said, doing his best to sound sad but failing. "The physician will be pleased by your efforts, Shannon. You have once again restored my brother to good health."

"She has the perfect touch," Rory said, a silky tone to his voice that made her glance twice at him.

Victor said nothing as he walked toward the door. "I shall see you in the morning. Sleep well, brother."

"And you."

When the door shut behind Victor, Shannon frowned at him. "You made it obvious you didn't want him here."

Rory shrugged. "Certainly you cannot blame me. He is worse than Mother ever thought of being. Plus, I want to be alone with my pretty caregiver."

His muscled abdomen clenched beneath her fingers as he moved, and she marveled at the power in his long, lean frame. He made her feel so impossibly female, and when his gaze settled on her, her pulse skittered.

"Let me see you," he said, his voice husky and sensual.

Heat rushed up her neck, staining her cheeks pink. With trembling hands, she unbuttoned her gown, slipped out of it and followed with the chemise.

Rory stared at her breasts and she could hear her heart roaring in her ears as she slid her drawers past her hips and stepped out of them.

"Lovely," he said, his eyes bright with a desire she recognized.

He slid off the bed, and lifted her in his arms. Her back was against the wall a second later. He lifted one of her legs over his hip and slid inside her with a low groan.

Would it always be like this between them, she wondered as he slowed his thrusts and kissed her passionately.

Her body tightened with each stroke, her tiny pearl brushing against him, sending a shiver down her spine.

He cupped her breasts, his breath hot on a nipple before he laved it with his tongue, drawing it deep into his mouth.

She was close to climax.

Rory grit his teeth and, lifted her up off the ground, using the wall as leverage.

As her hands tightened on his shoulders, he arched his hips and ground against her. She cried out in pleasure, and together they shot to the stars.

14

Each night for the rest of the week, Shannon slipped into Rory's room and they made love; then she would sneak back into her chamber before dawn. Although she was tired from lack of sleep, she was excited about her lover and could think of little else.

Except that she had not told Zachary about seeing Clinton or the gray-mustached gentleman in London.

Truth be told, she didn't want to leave. She was terrified of walking out those doors and never again seeing Rory.

Edward cleared his throat, folding his hands together. "A guest has joined Lord and Lady Graston for dinner, so please be especially vigilant and see to her every need."

A sense of foreboding washed over Shannon as she entered the dining room. A beautiful redhead with exotic light brown eyes sat directly across from Rory.

This must be Lady Kinkade, the widow Lady Rochester had spoke of.

The woman intended for Rory.

The lady looked up when Shannon approached, and her brows

furrowed, no doubt because Shannon had made eye contact. Having lived in a household that employed servants, she was well aware of the rule to remain invisible. And never, unless directly spoken to, look your betters in the eye.

Shannon managed to pour the lady tea without getting any on the lace tablecloth. When she finished, she poured for Victor, who sat to the lady's right, aware that Rory stared at her all the while.

Did he not realize how obvious he was being?

The widow looked at Shannon, her lips curving slightly before turning her full attention back to Rory.

Victor cleared his throat. "Lady Kinkade, I understand you have twin sons."

"Yes, they are five now."

"Did they come to London with you?"

Lady Kinkade smiled, obviously pleased by the interest in her children. "No, they stayed in Liverpool with my mother."

"Children are such a blessing," Lady Rochester said. "And nothing is better when those children grow up and find a loving spouse." She poured three heaping spoonfuls of sugar into her tea. "Sinjin and Victor have outdone themselves in their choice of brides, and I hope that Rory will follow suit."

Rory choked on the brandy he had just swallowed.

Lady Kinkade grinned. "You are most fortunate, Lady Rochester."

Lady Rochester nodded. "Indeed."

"I do hope you will be attending our little soiree at the end of the week," Lillith said to Lady Kinkade.

"Of course. Lady Rochester has invited me to stay on for the festivities."

Lillith's brows lifted in surprise. "How lovely."

Rory's jaw clenched tight and he glanced at his mother, who refused to make eye contact.

Shannon was only too happy to leave the dining room, even if it was to enter the kitchen where the other servants were talking about how beautiful Lady Kinkade was.

Worse still, everyone knew the woman was meant for Rory.

"Her husband was obscenely rich. Owned publishing houses throughout Europe," a maid said, lifting her brows high.

"Rich and beautiful—he should marry her before someone else does," a footman replied.

"Any man would pale in comparison to Lord Ambrose." This came from Candice, who had blurted the words and now blushed to the roots of her hair.

Two maids shared a smile that made Shannon wonder if perhaps they too hadn't slept with Rory. She was so foolish . . . hoping for something that could never be.

"Quit chatting and get the soup out," Edward said, irritation lacing his words. A no-nonsense personality, he had little tolerance for gossip.

Shannon picked up the silver tray and steadied herself for walking into the room again. Her hands trembled, the fine china clattering on the platter.

"Are you all right, Shannon?" Candice asked with a sympathetic smile.

"Yes, of course."

"I can trade with you, if you'd like." Candice motioned toward the heavier tray.

"No, I'm fine, thank you." Candice's duty was to refill each of the wineglasses, where Shannon only had to stand next to the server, who would be the one to serve the soup. The less interaction she had with Rory or Lady Kinkade, the better off she'd be.

"Thank you for your kind invitation to visit Claymoore Hall, Lady Rochester," Lady Kinkade was saying when she re-entered the room.

"Our family is happy to have you."

Shannon gripped the platter tight. Claymoore Hall? She was already being invited to the family's country home? At this rate, she would not be surprised if the banns were posted in the newspaper in the coming weeks.

Lady Kinkade had every quality a man of Rory's station could ask for. She was beautiful, wealthy, and had a sterling reputation, but unfortunately, he didn't want her. A shame since his mother was already smiling like the deed was done. Could she just not savor the fact she had already married off two sons and leave him in peace?

Beneath the table, his mother lightly stepped on his shoe. Apparently he was not conversing as much as she would like him to.

He reached for his glass and took another long drink.

"What do you like to do in your free time, Lady Kinkade?" Lillith asked, saving him from coming up with any questions.

Now, had she been Shannon, he would have asked her a hundred questions and still be interested in every answer.

"I do so enjoy archery and riding."

Rory glanced up from his soup. Lady Kinkade was looking right at him. "Lovely," he replied, and winced when his mother kicked him in the shin.

He forced himself not to look at Shannon, but it was difficult. That damn footman Johnny had been staring at her from the moment he walked into the room. The younger man made no effort at hiding his interest, and even now his gaze strayed to Shannon's chest.

"You will love Claymoore Hall, then," Victor said, steady smile in place. "The land is prime for riding and archery. . . . Though I must forewarn you, my brother is an ace with bow and arrow."

"Indeed, I have seen his prowess with my own eyes," Lillith remarked.

Rory sat up straighter in his chair. He always felt uncomfortable when others praised him.

"I am already impressed," Lady Kinkade said, biting into her lower lip.

He knew that look, could see the desire in those brown eyes. In fact, if he excused himself for a moment, she would do likewise. He could have her bedded and back at the table before the second course had been served. But he didn't want her. He wanted the mysterious servant with the haunted eyes.

"My family is too generous with their praise, Lady Kinkade," Rory said.

Victor snorted. "And my brother is too modest."

"A good trait," Lady Kinkade replied, wiping her mouth with her napkin.

By the time the main course was served, Rory wanted nothing more than to disappear to his chamber and make love to Shannon, but his mother had other plans. After listening to Lady Kinkade sing and play the piano, he was coerced into playing cards.

"You look tired, Rory," Lady Kinkade said with a concerned expression as she sat across from him at a small table. Everyone else conveniently found other activities to keep them occupied.

Rory glanced up at her. "Indeed, I am tired."

"You poor thing. I do so hope I didn't exhaust you too much," she said, looking truly distressed at the thought.

"Of course not."

She leaned in, exposing a good deal of creamy breast, no doubt her full intention. "I understand you were recently wounded in a duel," she whispered, her eyes widening. "I want to hear every detail."

His mother sat near the fire, knitting a sweater for her up-coming grandchild. She was too far away to hear the discussion, thank goodness. In her mind, if she didn't think about the duel, then surely it didn't happen.

"There is little to tell, Lady Kinkade."

"Please, call me Georgiana."

"Very well, Georgiana."

"And you killed the other man?" Her lips quirked. "I met Lord Cordland on several occasions, and I must say, I believe you did the lady a favor."

"I'm glad you approve."

"Oh, I approve." Given the throaty tone of her voice, he wondered what exactly they were speaking of.

"How are you doing, brother?" Lillith asked, coming up from behind him.

"I am well, Lillith."

Lillith tilted her head to the side. "I don't know. You look a bit piqued to me. Perhaps you should call it a night?"

Rory could have hugged her. "I think I might just do that, sister."

"We will see you at breakfast . . . if you are feeling up to it," she said, ignoring the frown that Georgiana threw her way.

"I shall see you tomorrow," Rory said to the other woman, whose gaze lingered in the vicinity of his crotch.

Rory said good night to his mother and Victor before walking in long strides to his chambers. He wondered if Shannon was in her room, asleep, or if she would be waiting for him in his bed.

He took the steps two at a time and rushed down the hallway. He stopped at the door of his chamber and realized his heart was pounding in anticipation. Dear Lord, she had gotten under his skin.

He opened the door and disappointment ate at his insides. The room was empty.

Shrugging out of his jacket and waistcoat, he then jerked his shirt from his pants, and reaching behind his head, pulled the shirt off and let it slide to the floor. "Damn it."

He raked his hands through his hair in frustration and sat on the end of the bed to remove his boots.

"Did you have a long night, my lord?"

His pulse skittered. Shannon stood at the doorway to the sitting room, her pale hair falling in long waves to her tiny waist. The chemise did little to hide the beautiful body beneath, and his body responded in kind.

"I didn't think you were going to come," he said, voicing his fears aloud.

"I thought it best to stay in the sitting room . . . just in case you brought someone else back with you."

Was that jealousy he heard in her voice? His lips curved, pleased that she, too, felt jealousy.

"I don't want Lady Kinkade, Shannon."

"She's beautiful."

"Not as beautiful as you."

Her brows furrowed and he could tell she didn't believe him. "She's wealthy."

"Yes, but I don't need money."

"Your mother seems quite determined."

"And my mother tried to convince my brothers to marry other women, but in the end, they married who they wanted, not who she wanted, and I shall do the same."

He pulled her close and kissed her, and his heart leapt when she leaned into him. Her hands moved to his chest, splaying there, over the steady pounding of his heart.

Shannon sighed, content to be in his arms at long last.

"I want you, Shannon. No one else. Just you."

She smiled against his lips, her arms tightening about his shoulders.

There was an insistent knock at the door, and Rory pulled back.

He frowned. "Bloody hell, it's probably just Victor . . . or Mother. I'll be just a second."

"Should I go to the sitting room?" she asked, alarmed at the possibility of being caught.

Knowing his mother, she would no doubt read him like a book and drag Shannon from the sitting room. "Perhaps the wardrobe would be better," he said, feeling horrible as he opened the door.

Shannon rushed toward the large cupboard across the room.

Rory took a deep breath, and sure that Shannon was clearly out of sight, he opened the door.

"Lady Kinkade." He did not hide the shock he felt upon seeing the woman at his chamber door.

15

Lady Kinkade's gaze settled on Rory's chest. "I was wondering if you could use some company tonight."

Wishing he'd had the foresight to slip his shirt back on, he crossed his arms over his chest. "I fear I am not feeling at all that well."

Her brows lifted high. "Come, Rory, your reputation precedes you. You never turn a woman away. If my friends find out, I shall be a laughingstock."

"Lady Kinkade . . ."

"Call me Georgiana," she insisted.

He forced a smile. "Georgiana, no one need know you were here."

She tilted her head slightly and her brows narrowed. "You have a woman in your room already, don't you?" she asked, her gaze scanning the room.

"Of course not."

"But why else would you be acting so suspiciously, Rory?" She said his name like a caress.

"I am recuperating from a wound, Georgiana. I am tired, and I am alone so that I can rest."

Her lips quirked. "And you, my lord, are a liar."

Irritated, he opened the door all the way. "See, I am alone."

To his surprise, she stepped past him into the room, and he cursed himself for his stupidity. She looked toward the sitting room, and with a saucy smile, rushed directly there and opened the door. Thank God Shannon had hidden elsewhere. He followed behind her, frustrated beyond all reason.

"Very curious," she said, walking toward him, her gaze scanning the room once more.

Obviously appeased, she didn't stop coming, and when she was in danger of stepping on his feet, he finally took a step back and his hip hit the mattress.

Her hands slid around his neck and she pressed her full breasts flush against him. "Come, Rory. I won't be long. We can make love and then you can sleep. I'll even rub your feet for you after."

"Georgiana, I am in no mood for company. My wound aches, and I feel feverish." He said the last on a whim, desperate for her to leave.

She pressed delicate fingers to the bandage. "Can I see the wound?" Her eyes lit up with excitement.

"No, my caregiver said it's important to keep it covered."

"Your caregiver is the pretty servant." She didn't phrase it as a question.

He nodded, wondering who had told her as much.

She bent down and kissed the bandage. "I will take care of you, Rory. If only you would allow me."

Shannon nearly bolted from the wardrobe and told both the woman and Rory to go to hell, but she was forced instead to bite her lip to keep from saying anything. Watching the man she was falling in love with being pawed by the beautiful blue-blood was a nightmare that she could not escape.

What must it be like to constantly have women throw themselves at you? she wondered, sweat beading on her forehead.

"Perhaps another time, Georgiana. My wound aches horribly tonight," Rory said once again in an attempt to thwart the lady, but she ignored him yet again and kissed him.

"I know something else that probably aches," she said, reaching for the band of his trousers.

He stilled her progress, his fingers wrapping around her wrist. His jaw clenched tight. "Georgiana, please."

She pushed him back onto the bed and was straddling him before Shannon could blink. Her breath caught in her throat as the other woman rotated her hips. "You do have a large one, don't you? Mmmm, I'm already wet."

Shannon gasped, then covered her hand with her mouth when Georgiana glanced toward the wardrobe. "Did you hear something?"

"It is probably a servant stoking the fire next door. Chances are he'll come here next," Rory said, sliding out from underneath Georgiana. "You should probably go."

Georgiana's brows furrowed; then she looked as though she would laugh as he stood and extended a hand to help her up.

Lady Kinkade flushed. "Well, I will take you at your word that you are too tired tonight. Your mother has invited me to stay on, so perhaps I can visit you tomorrow?"

The woman was unbelievable! Shannon's nails bit into her palms as she waited for Georgiana to leave. She just hoped she did so before Shannon passed out from heatstroke.

"Perhaps," Rory said, with a smile that Shannon could tell was forced.

Lady Kinkade's entire demeanor changed in the blink of an eye. "I must be a huge disappointment to you. Here I thought, given your reputation, you would want—"

Rory pulled the other woman close and kissed her.

Shannon bit her lip until she tasted blood. What was he doing? Did he forget she was in the wardrobe?

"That's much better," Georgiana all but purred against his lips.

"Until tomorrow," Rory said, walking her toward the door. She paused for one more kiss before he shut the door behind her.

Shannon wished she could blink her eyes and be in her small attic room, far away from Rory and Georgiana kissing.

She knew he did so in order to get her to leave, and perhaps to steer suspicion away from them, but to see him kissing the other woman was beyond excruciating.

He opened the wardrobe and she bounded out, straight for the chamber door.

"Wait, where are you going?"

"To bed."

"Shannon, stop," he said, pulling her against him, keeping her captive there.

She could feel his heart pound against her back. "I have to go."

"No, you don't."

"You kissed her." She wished she could take back the words the second she said them. They sounded so desperate, so envious, so childish.

"I had to. She knows I want you. She sees the attraction between us."

She turned in his arms, looked up into his intense blue eyes. "What are we doing, Rory?"

"I think it's obvious what we're doing," he said, the tone of his voice husky, and even more, she made the mistake of look-ing into those amazing eyes of his. The desire she saw there could not be misinterpreted. He lifted her chin with firm fin-gers, and his thumb brushed along her lower lip. "I want you. No one else. Just you, Shannon."

How many women had he said those same words to?

His hand slid down her neck, over the swell of her breasts, before cupping a globe. Her breath caught in her throat when his thumb brushed over a rigid peak.

"You don't want me, Shannon?" he asked, and she was stun-ned to see vulnerability in those blue depths.

Her gaze slid to the thick cords of his neck, to the fiercely beating pulse there, to the strong, wide chest. Without realizing it, she reached out and touched him, laying a hand flat against his heart. To her amazement, it raced, much like her own.

She licked her lips, looked up at him, and kissed him.

He let her take control, kissing her back, but waiting for her to set the pace. Excited, she ran her tongue along the seam of his lips and he opened to her.

Her tongue slid along his, tentatively at first. She cupped his face with her hands, deepened the kiss, and he groaned low in his throat, a primal sound that made the hair on her arms stand on end.

If he wanted her to take control, then so be it.

"Take off your pants," she said, shocking herself.

His eyes were heavy-lidded, and so incredibly sexy she had a difficult time remembering her name.

"As you wish." He unbuttoned his pants, shoved them past his hips, and followed with his drawers.

She swallowed past the sudden lump in her throat. How devastatingly beautiful he was, right down to his solid cock, jutting proudly from his body.

A shiver of excitement rushed through her, causing a throbbing at the juncture of her thighs.

"What of you?" he asked.

Slowly, she went to her knees before him, then took him into her mouth.

Satin over steel, velvet over stone. Such a delightful contrast, she thought, running her tongue along the thick, heavily veined cock. The plum-sized head was purple, and a tiny bead of fluid formed at the tip. She took him into her mouth and gripped the base as she pumped and sucked.

"Sweet Jesus," he said under his breath, and she hid a smile, knowing she must be doing something right.

He grew harder by the second, and she gloried in the power she felt, in seeing and feeling his reactions. Loving the way his chest expanded as he pushed her slightly away.

She went back on her heels and looked up at him. He was ready to climax. She could see the need in his eyes, feel his desire.

He lifted her right off her feet and tossed her onto the bed. She looked over her shoulder in time to see him standing behind her, cock standing at full attention, straining against his navel.

He reached up, grabbed hold of her waist, and pulled her toward him. Legs spread wide, he slid into her and she gasped at how stuffed she was by his cock, and the feeling of his balls as they settled against her as he cupped his hips.

Moving his hand beneath her, he stroked her clit and she groaned at the wonderful sensations rippling throughout her entire being.

She gripped the blankets as he slowly withdrew and then slid back in again.

Shannon's innocent touch had set his blood on fire, giving him a glimpse of the lover she was fast becoming.

Her snug quim hugged him tight, squeezing his thick length, pulling him in deeper with each stroke.

Flicking her clit with his fingers, she cupped her hips against his hand and heard the gasp at the same time her muscles throbbed around him and coated his length with her dew.

For his mother's benefit, Rory did his best to pretend interest in Lady Kinkade, but it was difficult with Shannon nearby. He was bewitched. Already he was hard just thinking about the next time they could be alone together.

"Sinjin and Kate will be meeting us at Claymoore Hall," his mother said to no one in particular as they walked beside the River Thames.

"How wonderful," Lillith replied, resting her head against her husband's arm. "How I miss my niece."

"And I miss my sister," Marilyn remarked.

Rory knew that he'd be going along to the family's country estate in the north soon, but only because Shannon would be traveling there with Lillith to attend to her.

If not for that reason, he would happily stay in London. He hoped the size of Claymoore Hall would allow ample opportunity for getting Shannon alone. A welcome change since he felt like his every move was being noted.

Perhaps time away would make her less skittish when it came to questions of a more personal nature. Whenever he asked her anything about her past, she conveniently changed the subject. And the image of the strange man following her in London still bothered him, but he had not questioned her about it.

A bird flew from a tree to perch on the nearby fence.

His gaze strayed to Shannon, who walked beside Marilyn. The two seemed exceedingly close, and he was glad to see her befriending the other woman. If only Shannon were of the gentry. Then perhaps he could make an offer for her hand.

The thought made him miss a step, and Victor frowned. "Are you all right?"

"Yes."

Victor looked skeptical. Until he was recovered, his brother would be hovering like a mother hen. Hell, even Betsy didn't show as much concern as his sibling about his injury. No, she was too busy worrying about potential brides.

Georgiana came up from behind him, slipping her hand around his elbow. "I shall keep you steady," she said with a wink. She wore a gown more suited for a ball, the green silk hugging her curves, and showing far more cleavage than was considered proper. He made sure to keep his gaze focused above her chin at all times as not to encourage her.

"Fetch my wrap," Georgiana said abruptly, looking toward Shannon.

It took Shannon a moment to realize Georgiana was speaking to her.

"Her name is Shannon," Rory said, keeping his voice even, but with great effort.

"Please, *Shannon*," Georgiana said, and Shannon nodded.

With chin lifted high, Shannon walked toward the manor, and it took everything he possessed not to follow her.

Ahead, Zachary and the growing irritant that was Johnny stood on the bank, setting up the chairs and table they had brought down from the house.

He'd like the opportunity to speak to the boy, but he needed to extract himself from Georgiana long enough to do so.

"I so wish this day was over. How I long for tonight," she whispered under her breath, looking up at him with seductive eyes.

Oh God. How in the world was he going to get out of this one?

"Ah, yes, I look forward to the dinner party. Lillith has a wonderful group of friends."

"That is not what I mean, and well you know it, my lord." She pressed her breast against his arm. "I dreamt of you last night."

Rory glanced at Victor, hoping his brother would help divert her advances, but he was laughing at something Lillith said.

Damnation.

"I've embarrassed you." She sounded surprised.

"I don't embarrass easily, Lady Kinkade."

"I thought I told you to call me Georgiana."

"Very well, Georgiana."

"Well, then, I shall be blunt." She glanced around, and making sure they were outside of hearing distance, said, "I was hoping that we could spend some time together this evening... after dinner. My room or yours?"

Last night telling her yes in order to get rid of her had seemed like the perfect solution. Now he was regretting it.

He slowly bent down and picked up a stone, and rolled it between his fingers. "This is my brother's house, where I am a guest, and it would not be right for me to entertain a lady in my chamber."

She laughed under her breath. "Come, Rory, you forget whom you speak to. You were just injured because you were making love to a woman within earshot of the entire dinner party. The women attending said they could hear Lady Cordland's heated moans through the thin walls. You had them all squirming in their chairs."

How utterly uncomfortable he was becoming. "Let's just say I have learned my lesson."

From the corner of his eye he saw Shannon, walking toward them with Georgiana's shawl in hand.

Her cheeks were tinged a flattering shade of pink from being in the sun. As she approached, she kept her gaze averted, until she helped Georgiana with the shawl. For an instant their gazes met, and his heart actually skipped a beat.

He remembered those lovely full lips of hers wrapped around his cock, her hot tongue licking him, and then the exquisite heat of her inner walls clamping tightly around him. Snug as a glove . . .

"Will there be anything else, Lady Kinkade?" Shannon asked dutifully, and the other woman forced a smile and shook her head.

"I think not. Thank you."

Shannon gave a curt nod and walked away, in the direction of her brother and Johnny.

16

Shannon grit her teeth and counted to ten twice. She could not stand that woman! Lady Kinkade was going out of her way to make Shannon feel uneasy and separate her from Rory.

It was agonizing to have to watch him court another woman right under her nose.

Zachary looked up from where he placed a tablecloth on the table he and Johnny had brought down to the river. The Scot grinned at her and brushed a hand through his unruly curls. "Good afternoon, Shannon."

"Good afternoon, Johnny."

"Might I say, you're looking beautiful today."

Zachary made a disgusted sound, but Johnny just laughed. "She is the loveliest lady I have ever seen."

"You are too kind, Johnny," she said with a smile.

"Will you go get the bottle of wine I left on the kitchen counter?" Zachary asked Johnny, and he nodded.

"Aye, but you owe me."

"Of course."

Zach waited until the other man was out of hearing range to turn to her. "Some of the servants are talking about ye."

Her stomach tightened. "What are they saying?"

"That you are having an affair with Lord Ambrose. Do not deny it, Shannon. Do not forget I saw ye with him."

"It is no one else's business what I do."

"What if you become pregnant with his child?".

A blush rushed up her neck to stain her cheeks. "It will not happen."

"Do not be stupid, sister. What would you do with a child? A bastard child? He or she would be one more mouth to feed. We barely have any money now."

He was right. She knew he was, and yet she knew it would be impossible to stay away from Rory.

"He will marry Lady Kinkade. She was sent here for that very reason. To continue is to put your heart in danger, and your own well-being."

Her heart was already in danger. She was falling in love with the notorious rakehell, and the longer she stayed here, the more under his spell she would become.

"I have feelings for him."

He brushed a hand down his face. "This is madness, Shannon. You know that it is. You are playing a dangerous game. One that you will not win. He is an aristocrat and you a servant. You know what the outcome will be. His brothers have both married within the space of weeks, and Lord Ambrose is next. We have all heard the ultimatum Lord and Lady Rochester gave all three of their sons."

She ignored this last and said, "But we really aren't servants, Zach. Our father built a dynasty, one that we should be heirs to."

"*Should be* is right, but we are not, Shannon." His voice was clipped and curt. "Do not think for a second that I don't wish the outcome were different. I hate that I must work my fingers to the bone for people that look down their noses at me."

"Lord and Lady Graston are good to us."

"Aye, they are, but I do not speak of them. These past months have been increasingly sobering, and I hate that I yearn for a future that will never be mine." Tears welled in his eyes and he blinked them away. "I am begging you to use your head, Shannon. Do not fall victim to his charm. He cannot give you what you need."

"Here ye are," Johnny said, and Shannon jumped, surprised he had returned so quickly.

The young man flashed a toothy smile and handed Zachary the bottle of wine.

"Thank you," Zachary managed, taking the bottle from him.

"Shannon, would ye mind helping me set the other table?" Johnny asked, picking up the linen tablecloth that he'd laid on a chair.

"Not at all," she said, only too glad to get away from the uncomfortable conversation she'd been having with her brother.

Johnny handed her a corner of the linen, his dark eyes dancing as he stared. He was so close, and she had to admit, she liked his easy charm. His shirt opened at the neck, showing a good expanse of chest hair and a silver necklace. "Will you be at the gathering tonight?"

"The gathering?"

"Aye, in the servants' hall after dinner is served. We are having a celebration for Candice and Frank's wedding. Lady Graston has given us all the evening off."

"How considerate of her."

"Indeed. I hope you will come."

"Of course I shall."

They placed the tablecloth and she smoothed it out, noting the way Johnny's gaze slid down her body. "I wish I would have known ahead of time. I would have bought something for them while I was in town."

"Do not concern yourself. It's enough that you are there."

"What of you?"

"I carved a little something for them," he said, pulling a smooth piece of wood from his pocket and handing it to her. Engraved into the side was a Celtic knot.

"It's a sign of eternal love."

"It's beautiful," Shannon said, running a finger over the intricate engraving.

"Ye see the loops are interwoven. There is no beginning and no end . . . just as love should be. That is what I hope for Frank and Candice. That their love lasts forever."

Would their love last forever? she wondered, remembering all too well how Candice had given herself to Rory. Already their relationship had faltered. Would it be the same with Shannon and Rory, especially now that Georgiana was here? Would the other woman win him over?

"They will love it, Johnny," Shannon said, handing the engraving back, and he beamed. His fingers lingered and she recognized the light in his eyes when she caught his gaze.

Rory cleared his throat and Shannon jumped.

He was still walking arm in arm with Georgiana, and as they approached the table, Johnny pulled out a chair for the lady.

Lady Kinkade sat beside Rory and even scooted her chair closer.

Shannon's nails dug into her palms, and Johnny followed her gaze. She did not miss his frown.

Rory would expect her to visit his room tonight, but if all the servants believed she was having an affair with the lord, she would be smart to stay away, at least for a night or so.

She knew Georgiana would be visiting him, and she wondered if, in her absence, he would sleep with the other woman.

Johnny took a step toward her and reached up to brush a wayward curl off her shoulder. The reaction was innocent, but she felt Rory's gaze on them. Was he as jealous of Johnny as she was of Georgiana?

Her gaze fell to his chest again, and she saw the corners of his mouth lift. "Your necklace is lovely," she said, embarrassed to have been caught staring. She didn't want him getting the wrong idea.

"I keep my mother's ring on it." He lifted the slender ring.

"She died?"

"Aye, she used to work for Lady Nordland." He shook his head, his hand falling back to his side. "I mean, Lady Graston. She died this past winter."

"I am sorry, Johnny. I know what it is to lose a parent."

"Aye, Zachary told me your parents died in a carriage accident last year."

Shannon swallowed hard. "Yes."

"Little wonder he doesn't want to drive the carriage any longer."

She nodded, hating the lies they were forced to tell. "The ring is beautiful, Johnny. I am sure your mother is glad you wear it so close to your heart."

"I like to believe she can see me. Do you think your parents see you?"

Shannon bit her bottom lip and nodded, "Aye, Johnny. I believe they do."

Looking over at Rory, she noticed he watched the exchange between herself and Johnny with interest, and she could clearly see the jealousy in his eyes.

* * *

Rory didn't know who he wanted to choke first, Shannon or Johnny. The two looked as thick as thieves, and it irritated him to no end. When the young man had lifted the lock of hair from her shoulder he had very nearly come out of his skin.

It hadn't helped that Georgiana had giggled under her breath, far too aware of his frustration.

Three glasses of whiskey later and his irritation was not improving. His brother walked along the edge of the water with his wife, and his mother sat in her chair, reading a novel, and watching the happy couple with a smile. Is this how it was going to be for the unforeseeable future, forced into keeping Lady Kinkade busy? His mother's trap would push him to an early grave.

He was almost relieved when dark clouds rolled in overhead. His mother, who could never tolerate the cold, stood and slipped the book in the pocket of her gown. Victor and Lillith also started toward the house.

A crack of thunder sounded on the horizon, and Georgiana stood. "It is time for us to return to the manor. Perhaps I can interest you in a game of chess, my lord?"

"I think I shall be taking a nap," he replied, covering a forced yawn for full effect.

She frowned and looked skeptical.

"Perhaps we can play before dinner."

She instantly brightened. "I accept." She slid her hand around his elbow and they walked toward the manor.

They parted company inside, and Rory walked up the steps to his room, closing the chamber door behind him and rushing toward the window.

He could see the servants working feverishly to bring back the tables and chairs. Shannon had taken the linens and bunched them in a ball that she carried in her arms. Fat raindrops fell on her, but she did not seem to mind. In fact, the servants went about their business, oblivious of the weather.

Shannon's gown clung to her body, and he could see the outline of her slender legs, remembering well those creamy thighs spread wide as she took him into her body.

Not wanting to be seen, he took a step back.

Johnny said something to Shannon that made her laugh, and Rory felt overcome with jealousy.

What the hell was the matter with him? It was not like him to feel envy toward any man, but he felt a possessiveness toward Shannon that bordered on obsession.

She was his. He didn't want anyone else touching her, or even making her laugh.

The group disappeared into the house, and he waited, undecided on what to do. Would she come to him? Maybe it would have served him better had he not recovered so quickly, because then she would still be his caregiver. But aside from growing tired, his shoulder had mended well, and there was no need to keep the bandage on, as it was healing nicely.

He paced the room, watching the clock on the mantel tick away the minutes. "Bloody hell," he said under his breath after ten minutes came and went. He left his chamber, heading down the servants' stairwell, having no desire to see his brother, Lillith, Marilyn, his mother, or God forbid, Georgiana.

Passing by one servant who gasped and stopped like a scared rabbit until he passed, Rory wondered if he hadn't lost his mind just a little. Perhaps he was getting feverish?

Slipping onto the floor of the servant's quarters, he went to Shannon's room and, instead of knocking, walked in.

She turned, her eyes wide.

Wearing nothing but a soaking wet chemise, she stared at him. He closed the door and leaned against it.

Pink nipples strained against the sheer fabric, and he could see that shadow outlined the juncture of her thighs.

She licked her lips. "Rory, what are you doing?"

"I had to see you."

"But I must change and get downstairs. Cook has asked for my assistance in the kitchen."

"Perhaps I should ask Lillith to promote you to lady's maid."

"I do not seek your assistance." Her tone was clipped, and he realized she was angry with him.

"Come here," he said, but she didn't budge.

He frowned. "Then I shall come to you."

He approached her and she actually took a step back. "My brother tells me that the servants are talking."

"Is that why you flirt with Johnny?"

Her brow furrowed. "Flirt with Johnny? I was not flirting with him. We were talking."

"You were doing more than talking. He was showing you something." When she remained quiet, he said, "Are you trying to make me jealous?"

"I didn't think I could ever make you jealous."

"You are wrong." He cupped her jaw, his thumb brushing over her cheek, before his fingers raked through her hair. His lips were inches from hers, and he looked deep into her beautiful eyes. "I ache to possess you completely. I want you. I do not care what others say. Let them talk. Let them say what they will."

She closed her eyes, and he kissed each lid. She had not responded to him at all. In fact, her arms remained at her sides.

"Do you want me to leave, Shannon?"

She opened her eyes. He could see the inner war playing out behind those blue depths. She shook her head slowly. "No. No, I don't."

Her arms encircled his neck, and she went up on her toes to kiss him. He slid the chemise off her shoulders until it fell to her ankles in a puddle.

"You're so cold. Let me warm you," he said, holding her tight to his body, savoring the feel of her limbs flush against him.

"Your shoulder," she said, easing back.

"It only pains me a little."

Shannon could see the need in his eyes. Feel the evidence of his desire pressed against her thigh.

"In the chair," he whispered against her lips.

She sat down, and he nudged her thighs apart. Going down on his knees between them, his hot breath fanned her sex, and her stomach tightened as he leaned in and gently licked her.

Her breath left her in a rush and she gripped his shoulders as his tongue worked its magic, sliding over her sensitive folds, lifting the tight bundle of nerves, toying it relentlessly until she was arching against his mouth, craving more.

Rory eased her legs over his shoulders, giving him better access. He licked her over and over again, sliding his tongue into her snug passage.

She gripped his head, her nails grazing his scalp.

He sucked hard on her clit and she cried out, her quim throbbing and pulsing against his mouth.

She looked down at him, and his breath lodged in his throat. The heated look had him easing her up onto her feet.

Gripping the back of the chair for support, she groaned as his cock nudged her soaking entrance. He slid inside her slowly, his hands cupping her breasts, rolling taut nipples between thumbs and forefingers.

He pinched lightly, pulling the peaks into tight little buds.

One hand slid down her firm belly, through the downy hair that covered her sex, sliding over her clit.

Her breath lodged in her throat as the exquisite pressure began to build deep inside her. With each stroke she came closer and closer to the pinnacle that would push her over the edge.

Rory felt her coming closer to orgasm and held on until her inner muscles clamped down around him. He gripped her hips and pumped against her, until his own release came.

17

Georgiana had been walking toward Rory's chamber when she saw him exit his room.

She had nearly called out to him, but curious, especially since he'd said he was so tired, she had followed him.

All the excitement she'd been feeling these past hours faded when she saw him enter the servants' staircase. Her stomach fell to her toes. She should have known. He had not been able to keep his eyes off the little servant all afternoon. Indeed, when Shannon had flirted with the handsome footman, the nerve in his jaw had jumped and he had clenched his teeth tight together.

Waiting a few minutes, she followed him into the servants' corridor, and hearing the door open and close, she went to the very next room, which was thankfully empty.

Placing an ear against the door, she heard movement in the next room. She heard voices, but they were hardly more than a murmur.

She could not afford to lose Rory as a possible suitor. The alternative was extremely sobering, and she was disappointed that the only suitors who had approached were much older men.

Plus, she wanted a husband who excited her. A handsome man who made her yearn for the bedchamber. And Rory fit the criteria in more ways than one.

She wanted to be the envy of all her friends. Wanted the room to go silent when they walked in. Everyone would know who she was then.

But she would not get a ring on her finger by playing the demure widow. Lord how she had tried to get his attention, but it was nearly impossible under this roof with a certain angelic-looking servant with startlingly beautiful eyes.

The adjoining room went silent; then she heard a feminine moan and the slight screeching of a chair. An image came to mind and she pushed it away, but when she heard a steady rocking follow, she knew what was happening. She was tempted to pound on the wall. Yet how would she possibly explain herself when Rory walked in, and he would certainly come over, irritated beyond reason that he had been interrupted fucking his little servant.

Her body burned as she continued to listen to the lovers have sex.

It had been only weeks since the house party where she'd played a dangerous game of cat and mouse with Lord Hendley, a long-married man and figurehead in Parliament, and husband to her best friend. She knew he'd be discreet, and he had been, coming to her room at three in the morning. The sex had been underwhelming, but it had scratched an itch for the time being and helped heal the wound her lover had left when he'd walked out the door.

Lord Hendley had never asked to see her again, and it had been a blow to her ego. She had left his household wiser. Since then Lady Hendley had asked her to visit again, and she had readily refused.

A mingling of cries sounded in the other room. Long minutes passed, then finally she heard the door open and close. She cracked the door open, looked out, and saw Rory walking down the hallway.

Her stomach tightened.

She had her work cut out for her. The man was truly besotted with the little slut.

The servants' hall was lit with candles, and as Floyd played the fiddle and one of the footman a flute, the servants joined into a line and danced.

Shannon clapped along with the others as Candice, with her crown of daisies, held hands with Frank and rushed down the line of dancers who had made an archway with their bodies.

"Come on, Shannon," Johnny said, taking hold of Shannon's hand.

"I haven't danced in ages," she said, but he didn't care. He laughed as they joined the others. The last time she had attended a dance had been in Dublin a good nine months before. She'd been tutored in dance since the age of five, so she was not a stranger to the steps. Johnny was light on his feet as well, and she found herself having a wonderful time, laughing with the others, clapping in time to the music.

All night Johnny had been attentive to her every need, making sure she had punch, not leaving her side. He was a sweet boy, and she felt guilty knowing she could not return his affection. It was impossible because Rory held her heart.

God help her, but she had truly gotten herself into a mess of her own making. Guilt ate her every time she saw Zachary, who at the moment danced with the scullery maid. Like her, he seemed to be enjoying himself immensely, laughing and clapping in time to the music.

The dance ended abruptly and they all clapped their hands. "Would ye like to get some fresh air?" Johnny asked.

She was warm, and the room had grown stuffy. "Sure," she replied, following him outside.

Because of the recent rain, the air was clean and brisk and felt wonderful against her flushed skin. "Ye are a wonderful dancer, Shannon," Johnny said, white teeth flashing in the moonlight.

"Thank you, Johnny. And you are as well."

He took a step closer and Shannon straightened. Perhaps she ought not to have come outside with him. "I like ye, Shannon. Ye know that, don't ye?"

Oh dear. She nodded, afraid of where the conversation would lead.

Another step and he was within arm's reach. She took a quick step back, lost her balance, and would have ended up on her bum if not for Johnny grabbing her about the waist.

"Are ye all right, lass?" he asked, pulling her close. She could feel the unsteady hammering of his heart against her chest, along with the unmistakable stiffness of his anatomy.

Rory followed Georgiana out onto the verandah and down the pathway that led along the side of the manor house. "Where are we going?"

"It is a surprise," she said, a wide smile on her lips.

Dinner had ended two hours before, and he had spent the better part of those two hours in a card game with Victor and his mother. Georgiana had talked to Lillith for a while, and he had thought when she disappeared earlier that perhaps she had decided to retire for the night.

Apparently he'd been wrong.

Hearing music, he glanced at Georgiana.

"They are having a party," she said with a coy smile.

"The servants?"

Shannon had not said anything about a party, and he had

noted that Edward had been the only servant attending after dinner.

Intrigued, he followed her up the pathway.

The windows to the servants' hall had been opened, and the music slipped out into the night. Laughter and voices were raised in joviality and he could not help but smile.

"They certainly know how to make merry, do they not?" Georgiana said, as they approached the window.

The majority of the group was dancing, including a certain blond-haired servant who positively beamed at her handsome partner.

Rory felt like he'd been socked in the stomach, and now he knew why Georgiana had brought him here. She wanted him to see Shannon with Johnny.

As Shannon and Johnny took hands and strolled down the line of dancers, he felt more than a tinge of envy toward the young man.

Why had she not told him about the party? he wondered.

The dance ended and Johnny took Shannon's hand and they walked out the door. Rory was in an awkward position. He had never been the type of man to snoop, and he felt strange doing so now, and yet when Georgiana kept walking down the pathway and stopped at the corner of the house to spy on the two, he caught up with her.

Georgiana put a finger to her lips.

He hesitated, then stopped behind her, glancing over her shoulder at the two. He could not hear their discussion, but when the boy took a step toward Shannon and she faltered, he nearly stormed toward them, but Georgiana held tight to him and shook her head.

The music started up again, a slow tune that Rory didn't recognize. Johnny took Shannon in his arms and they were dancing, close together, in each other's arms, her hand on his shoulder, one clasped firmly in the man's other hand, while Johnny's fingers nearly encompassed her tiny waist.

Mine. Everything within him screamed the single word.

The two looked like lovers in a quiet moment. A romantic moment, and Rory was reminded that all he'd had with her were stolen moments, but those stolen moments had nothing to do with romance.

Ironically, most of his liaisons had been similar, quick couplings, with nothing romantic about them. He remembered earlier today how the two had their heads together looking at something. Rory had caught a quick glimpse of the engraving, of which Shannon had seemed truly fascinated.

Rory had skill when it came to archery, boxing, hunting, and fencing, but when it came to a hobby in terms of artistic ability, he lacked in all ways.

Johnny leaned Shannon back, following her with his body, his mouth hovering above hers, and Rory saw red.

The servant as quickly let her up. Shannon laughed as he spun her in a fast circle and then rested her forehead against his shoulder.

Rory clenched his teeth. He'd had enough of this.

Georgiana squeezed his hand and he looked at her.

There was a light in her eyes that had been missing before, and was that the slightest curving of her lips?

"Come, let us leave them to their little party," she said, and started walking back up the path.

He turned back to the couple, still dancing in the small courtyard under the moon. Shannon's laughter cut through him like a knife through butter.

Betrayal was not an emotion he was familiar with, and now it burned within him like a fire raging out of control.

18

Marilyn made her way through the throng of guests to her aunt's side. She had not realized so many people would be attending the dinner party. At least luck was with her, because Lady Anna had yet to make an appearance.

"Hello, my dear," Aunt Lillith said, kissing Marilyn on each cheek. "How lovely you look in that new silk frock. I told you that the color would make your eyes even more prominent."

"Thank you, Aunt Lillith. You do spoil me so."

"And I enjoy spoiling you," Lillith said. "And speaking of spoiling you, where is Stanley? I thought he would be here by now."

"He will be late. He had a business matter to attend to." Marilyn had noted the one negative quality about her betrothed was that he was constantly tardy. Thank goodness what he lacked for in punctuality he made up for in kindness. And Lord knows he loved her. He told her as much just yesterday. It had been an awkward moment, made worse still when she could not reciprocate and return his sentiment. Yes, she cared for him, but love . . . she wasn't so sure about.

"Ah, he must have heard us talking, for there he is," Lillith said, motioning to Stanley, who upon seeing them, brightened immediately.

He was dressed in an expensive navy suit that fit him well, and Marilyn felt a little spike of pleasure rush through her as he approached.

"How he adores you," Lillith said, sounding pleased.

Stanley rushed to her side. "You are angry with me," he said, and Marilyn could not be cross with him.

The well-practiced lecture on punctuality died on her tongue when the double doors to the parlor opened and Lady Anna appeared on the arm of a tall man with auburn hair. Dressed in a handsome suit, and with his hair swept off his forehead, he cut a dashing figure. Where had she seen him before?

"Do you know her?" Stanley asked.

Aunt Lillith followed his gaze. "Ah, yes, that is Lady Anna."

"Lady Anna. I have heard her name before."

Marilyn felt her cheeks grow warm. No doubt he had heard the rumors that circulated through London of late. It was impossible to go anywhere without hearing about her scandalous interludes with multiple partners.

"We met Lady Anna at Claymoore Hall, didn't we, Aunt Lillith?" Marilyn blurted, trying with difficulty to ignore the racing of her heart.

"Indeed, we did," Lillith replied. "She's a delightful young lady."

"I should very much like to meet her," he said, kissing her fingers. "For any friend of yours is a friend of mine."

He was such a passionate man, so kind and good to her. She savored the kisses they had shared and the few heated moments. In fact, on more than one occasion she had very nearly given him her maidenhead, if only to prove to herself that what she felt for Anna was wrong, but she stopped short of doing so.

She would wait until her wedding night and Stanley had agreed, but there had been no denying the passion in his eyes.

"Here comes your friend now," Stanley said excitedly.

Marilyn straightened and tried to calm her nerves. They had not seen one another since the ill-fated carriage ride where Marilyn had denied Anna's advances, and the letters Anna had written to Marilyn had gone unanswered. She had read only one, and it had been a flirtatious correspondence that hinted at getting together very soon.

Marilyn's heart was a roar in her ears as Anna stopped before her.

"My dear friend, how I have missed you while you've been away," Anna said.

Marilyn forced a smile and hoped that Stanley could not read through her nervousness. "How very kind of you to say, Lady Anna," she replied in a high-pitched voice.

Anna's lips quirked as she glanced from Marilyn to Stanley.

Marilyn could feel Stanley's gaze on her, and she glanced up at him. "Forgive me. How rude. Stanley, I would like for you to meet my friend Lady Anna. Lady Anna, this is Lord Sutton, my fiancé."

Anna's brow lifted. "Fiancé, oh yes, that's right," she said, her lips curving in a smile that looked almost genuine. "Congratulations to you both, and what a pleasure it is to meet the man who has stolen my Marilyn's heart."

The way she said "my Marilyn" was altogether too intimate, and Stanley pursed his lips together as he glanced between Marilyn and Anna.

He cleared his throat. "It is a pleasure to meet you as well, Lady Anna," Stanley said, suddenly looking like a proud peacock. "I was just telling Marilyn that any friend of hers is a friend of mine."

"How very sweet," Anna said with a coy smile.

"My husband is motioning for me to join him," Lillith said. "Please excuse me. So good to see you, Lady Anna. I'm so very glad you could join us this evening."

"I wouldn't have missed it for the world, Lady Graston," Anna replied.

Marilyn glanced at Stanley. "Would you mind getting me a glass of punch? I am parched."

"Of course, my dearest," he said, his gaze shifting to Anna. "Would you like a glass as well, Lady Anna?"

"Yes, thank you," she replied, watching as Stanley walked off, her gaze lingering too long on his backside to suit Marilyn's tastes.

"He is such a sweet boy, though a bit too stiff, if you ask me."

"I did not ask you," Marilyn said in a gruff voice.

Anna lifted her brow. "Come, Marilyn. Let there be no harsh feelings between us."

When Marilyn didn't respond, Anna said, "I am glad you are back, Marilyn. You have no idea how much I have truly missed you."

"Thank you. It is nice to be back."

"You are living with your aunt now?"

"Yes, while my mother is in Greece."

"When does she return?"

"By January . . . right before my wedding."

Anna smelled incredible, a combination of lavender and vanilla that made Marilyn's heart skip a beat.

Anna licked her carefully rouged lips and leaned toward Marilyn. "Meet with me in private or I shall die."

Marilyn straightened her shoulders, stunned at the blunt statement. "We have gone through this before, Anna. My feelings have not changed."

"The eyes do not lie, Marilyn. I believe you feel something for me."

Was her attraction to the woman obvious to others? "I am spoken for, Anna."

Something Marilyn couldn't distinguish flashed in the other woman's brown eyes but was gone a second later. "Perhaps you will reconsider." She leaned closer, her lips nearly brushing Marilyn's neck. "Just one night, Marilyn."

The temptation to say yes was incredible, for since the day she had met Anna at Claymoore Hall, the woman had left a mark on Marilyn's heart.

She had not dreamt that she would be attracted to a woman in a physical way, and yet when Anna had kissed her that night at Claymoore Hall, she had felt an overwhelming sense of excitement that could not be denied.

"I will not be unfaithful to Stanley."

Anna sighed heavily. "You are not married yet, Marilyn."

True, but soon she would be, and if she did anything now, she would feel extreme guilt.

Stanley was too good to her, and he knew the truth about her past, knew that she was a bastard and not the true daughter of Lord Melton. And he still wanted her. Wanted her because he said he loved her.

"Perhaps it is time for you to find a husband," Marilyn said, glad to see Stanley making his way back toward them.

"Actually, there is a gentleman I am considering. He is an American, and my grandmother is very excited about him."

"Will you move to America?" Marilyn asked, trying hard to ignore the pain she felt at the notion of Anna moving an ocean away. What was wrong with her? She should be jumping for joy.

"Yes, I would. He lives in Virginia. A wealthy plantation owner."

"I see."

Anna lifted her chin. "I think the change would be good for me. After all, I have grown weary of England. Do not get me wrong, I shall always consider England home, but I would very much like to see the vastness of America. I understand it is easy to start over, and Lord knows that would not hurt me."

Anna's reputation was scandalous, and it would be rare for her to find a man in England who was not acquainted with her sordid past. Even a foreigner would find out about her if he came to England. As though reading Marilyn's mind, Anna said, "My grandmother has planned a trip to Virginia this next spring."

Spring was an awfully long way away.

"Here we are, ladies," Stanley said, handing Anna a cup of punch and Marilyn the other.

A bell sounded in the dining room and the room fell silent.

"Ladies and gentlemen, please be so kind as to follow us to the dining room," Victor said, and with Lillith on his arm, he escorted the guests into the dining room.

"I had better find my companion," Anna said. "It was a pleasure meeting you, Lord Sutton."

"You as well, Lady Anna. I am sure that I shall be seeing more of you now that Marilyn is back in London."

Anna smiled, her gaze falling on Marilyn. "You can count on it."

By the time Marilyn took her seat, the majority of the other guests had been seated and were already conversing, including Lady Anna's companion.

The handsome young man with auburn hair flashed her a warm smile. "Good evening."

"Good evening. I am Lady Marilyn, Lady Graston's niece."

"Ah, yes, my friend Lady Anna talked about you. I am Clinton O'Connor."

Her pulse skittered and she wondered exactly what Anna had told him about her. Feeling trapped by his gaze, she reached out, grabbed her drink, and lifted it to her lips. "O'Connor. Are you Irish?"

"Indeed, I am."

"How long have you known her? Lady Anna, that is. Have we met before?"

"I think not. I only arrived in London this last week. I met Lady Anna at a soiree and she was kind enough to take me under her wing and introduce me to some of her friends, including your aunt's brother-in-law, Lord Ambrose."

"How very kind of her."

She was saved from having to make further conversation when the door opened from the kitchen and servants appeared dressed in formal black, carrying silver trays with steaming bowls.

Among the servants was Shannon, her platinum hair twisted in a knot. Even dressed in simple attire, her beauty could not be ignored. Marilyn glanced at Rory, and though he tried to keep from staring, he was struggling, and Lady Kinkade had noticed.

The widow had pulled out all the stops, wearing expensive jewelry and dressed in a stunning scarlet and gold silk dress that put everyone else's gowns to shame.

You wouldn't know it, though, by Rory's lack of interest.

Apparently Shannon had caught more than just Rory's eye. Beside Marilyn, Clinton sat up straighter as he stared directly at Shannon.

She, in turn, glanced in Clinton's direction and very nearly walked right into the back of the servant who was in front of her.

19

Shannon was stunned. The last person she had expected to see at the dinner party was her cousin. And yet there he sat, directly beside Lady Marilyn, looking every bit at ease as any of the many bluebloods at the table.

The murdering wretch.

Trembling, she forced herself to calm down and tightened her grip on the wine carafe.

"Are ye all right, lass?" Johnny asked beside her, and she nodded.

Her worst fears had been realized. Clinton had indeed found them, and he had them cornered. There was nowhere to go.

Even more, she had not forewarned her brother of the impending danger. Had Zachary seen Clinton already, or had he been too busy? She would not get a break for the rest of the evening and by then it would be too late. Clinton would be leaving and would possibly see Zachary, and then what would he do? Kill him right there and flee? Certainly he wouldn't when there were so many other people here. What did he plan, then?

Oh dear God, what had she done? She had not been honest with her brother, and all because she had been afraid that he would insist they leave, and she could not bear to leave Rory.

Rory, the man who made her blood burn, the man she loved. She could feel his stare burning into her, but she could not look at him for fear of what he would see in her eyes.

Fear. And Lord knows he could read her easily enough as it was. He would know in an instant that something was horribly wrong.

She glanced at her cousin. Clinton's face showed no emotion whatsoever. Just cold indifference.

Someone snapped their fingers and she realized that a guest was trying to gain her attention.

"Stay alert, lass," Johnny said, looking genuinely concerned about her.

It was Shannon's duty to keep wine in each of the guests' glasses, and she approached the portly man who had snapped at her.

Shannon steadied her hands enough to pour the wine without getting any on the table. The man watched her the entire time, his odd body odor making her hold her breath.

She kept an eye on the glasses, and saw that her cousin gulped down his wine. Thankfully, she was assigned to serve the guests on the opposite side of the table, but that did not stop Clinton from taunting her.

He sat back in his seat watching her closely, as though he was daring her to meet his gaze.

Shannon's gaze skipped to Marilyn. The young woman glanced at her and then looked to Clinton. She reached for her wineglass and took a drink.

Soon enough the carafe was empty, and Shannon was heading back into the kitchen. On the other side of the door she released the breath she hadn't realized she'd been holding.

She didn't want to go back in there. She had to get to her brother before Clinton did.

Candice walked in. "Are you all right, Shannon?" she asked again. "You're trembling like a leaf."

"I need to see my brother."

She frowned. "All right. I suppose I can cover for you, but do not be long."

"Thank you, I'll hurry."

Rory's fingers tightened around the goblet as he watched Anna's dinner companion, the over-friendly Clinton O'Connor, stare at Shannon. His sharp interest seemed to be bothering her, too, because she was much more nervous than usual.

"Your friend is being incredibly rude," Rory said to Anna, wiping his lips with his napkin. "I am two seconds away from knocking his nose into his skull."

Anna laughed under her breath. "You noticed his interest in your little lover, I see," she said, a wicked smile on her lips that slowly faded when she saw he was serious about his threat.

"Oh dear, you do like this one. It is not like you to be intimidated by any man."

His feelings for Shannon ran deep, and he need not be reminded of his sudden insecurities.

Rory thought of the mysterious man following her in London the other day and wondered if there might be a connection.

Shannon knew Clinton. That much was certain by her reaction. But who was he to her? A jilted betrothed, he thought with a sickening feeling to his stomach. Or perhaps an ex-employer who had been swindled by her brother?

No, the two hardly appeared to be thieves. Plus, he couldn't envision any employer following servants across an ocean.

He feared of what the connection might be, and given Shannon's reaction, it was probably the first. A jilted betrothed who had been cast aside.

A myriad of emotions rushed through him at the thought of another man laying claim to her. She belonged to him, and he would fight for her.

Shannon found Zachary leaning against a post, smoking a cheroot. Obviously shocked to see her, he dropped the tobacco and crushed it with his heel. "Shannon, what are ye doin? I thought you were serving tonight."

"Clinton is here."

His eyes widened in alarm and he made a strange, strangling sound. He looked toward the house and raked a hand through his hair. "Oh my God. He is attending the dinner party?"

"Yes."

"How could this have happened?"

She closed her eyes and took a deep breath.

"What are ye not telling me, Shannon?" He gripped her arms. "You knew he was here all along?" His voice was incredulous.

"Aye, I saw him while I was in London . . . while we were shopping the other day."

"You saw him and ye said nothing?" He released her as though her touch had burned him. "What the hell? We could have been long gone from here."

"I'm sorry, Zach."

"Sorry will not save us now, will it? He will find us, to be sure. I've no doubt."

Dear God, what had she done?

"What if we tell Lord Graston? Certainly he will protect us."

"Lord Graston is a good man, but Clinton is one of them now. He has managed to claw his way into Society, and who do you think they will believe? Us, a couple of servants on the run, or him, a rich businessman?"

"He is rich from our father's wealth."

"Do you think it matters to any of those people in there where his money comes from?" he said, motioning toward the manor.

"I'm sorry," she said again, but Zachary shook his head.

"Bloody hell, what is wrong with ye? Have you lost all sense of self?" His eyes narrowed. "Dear God, it's because of Lord Ambrose. You didn't tell me because ye did not want to leave him."

There was no sense in denying the accusation. "It's not just Lord Ambrose. I was tired of running. I was happy here. I *am* happy here."

"As am I, but for God's sake, Shannon, I would have at least liked the opportunity to have survived this. Instead, my own sister betrays me."

He may as well have slapped her. "Then let us leave now," she whispered.

"We are not prepared, and he would follow. No, we must outwit him." He ran a hand down his face. "Return to the dining room. Do not let on that anything is amiss. Stay where everyone can see ye, particularly Lord Ambrose. He will not let anything happen to ye."

"And what of you?"

"I can look after myself. I will stay near Floyd and Johnny."

"Can you not have another groom step in and take your place?"

"He knows I am here, Shannon. What sense does it make in hiding? He will find me no matter what. Remember, there is safety in numbers."

"We can leave," she said again, but he shook his head.

"He would only have us followed. He has others out watching us. I've little doubt that someone is watching now."

She swallowed hard.

"We will wait and see what he does."

"I fear for you. You sleep in the stables."

"The door is kept locked at night."

But she would not put it past her cousin to break the lock. Or what if he set fire to the stables? she thought, feeling sicker by the minute. "Ye had better return before your absence is noted."

She nodded and started back toward the house, tears clogging her throat. Her selfishness might have caused her own demise, and that of her brother's too.

"Shannon," he shouted, and she turned back to look at him.

"Be careful."

She nodded. "You too."

Her heart pounded in time with her steps as she approached the servants' entrance. She reached for the door handle when a hand reached out and grabbed her.

Oh dear God.

"What are you doing, Shannon?"

She released an unsteady breath. "Rory, you scared me." She had not seen him all day and could not help the feelings of guilt that raged through her now. Last night Johnny had been so kind to her, and she had enjoyed his company, but she could not help but feel like she was being unfaithful to Rory.

"I couldn't help but notice your replacement at dinner. I was worried."

"I had to talk to Zachary."

His brows furrowed and his eyes searched hers. "It must have been urgent if it couldn't wait until after dinner."

She hated lying to him and wished more than anything she

could be honest. "I heard he was not feeling well, so I went to see for myself."

"And how is he faring?"

"He is going to speak to Floyd and see if he can take the rest of the night off."

"A good idea. Perhaps you should take the rest of the night off as well."

She nodded. "Perhaps."

His eyes were so intense it was difficult to keep his gaze. He tilted his head slightly. "Who is Clinton O'Connor to you, Shannon?"

She did her best to school her features. "Who?"

"The redheaded gentleman seated beside Marilyn. The man who makes you so nervous. You clearly know him from somewhere."

She shifted on her feet. "The only reason I am nervous is because he stares . . . and that makes me uncomfortable."

His eyes narrowed. "Why do I feel you are keeping something from me?"

She dropped her gaze to his cravat. Why did she feel like they were not only speaking about Clinton?

"Tell me, Shannon."

It was difficult to remind herself that she hadn't known Rory for all that long, and that he could be out of her life as easily as he had come into it.

With a muttered curse, he pulled her into the house; then he kissed her, deeply, his mouth relentless. Her arms slid around his strong shoulders and she clung to him. He made all her senses go awry.

His hands moved down her back, over her buttocks, where he pulled her tight against his huge erection. It had been twenty-four hours since they'd last made love, and yet it felt like an eternity.

Moaning against her mouth, he pulled away the slightest bit. "I wish I could stay here with you, but I must return."

"As do I."

"No, I will tell Lillith and Victor that you retired for the night. Go there and do not leave. Come to my room at midnight."

She melted against him, wishing more than anything that he could take her far, far away from here. She knew that time was ticking, that she and Zachary would have to leave soon.

20

Clinton O'Connor stayed by Anna's side the rest of the night. The couple sat on a settee in a far corner of the parlor where the majority of Lillith and Victor's guests mingled. Though he played a game of chess, he seemed rather preoccupied with the comings and goings of the household servants, his gaze riveted on the parlor door.

As long as he knew where the Irishman was, Rory could rest easy that Shannon was all right. It would be a gutsy move to stroll through a stranger's home looking for a servant.

Marilyn approached him. "So I was not the only one who noticed the Irishman's keen interest in Shannon."

Rory glanced at her. "You did as well?"

She nodded. "You know, when I was shopping with Aunt Lillith and Shannon the other day, Shannon had a very odd re-action. She was looking at her reflection in the mirror and I was standing right behind her. Her gaze shifted slightly—to something or someone—and she gasped."

"Did you see who it was that startled her?"

"No, but earlier I had noticed a young man watching us, but I did not think anything of it. After all, men are known to stare, but tonight when I met Clinton, he seemed familiar to me. And not familiar in a sense that we'd been introduced, but that I'd seen him somewhere. It took me until just now for it to come together."

Rory's pulse skittered. "There was a man in London that day. An older man with silver hair and a thick mustache. Victor and I saw him following you."

Marilyn frowned. "In the tea shop?"

"Yes, Victor and I were across the street and we saw him follow you out of the shop. When you stopped at the stationery store, he waited outside and watched you from the street."

She gave a shiver. "You're scaring me."

Anna stood and walked toward them, leaving her companion behind.

"Let me know if I can help," Marilyn added.

"Thank you," he said, just as Anna approached them.

Anna smiled. "We are going to leave shortly, but I was hoping to have a word with you first," she said to Marilyn.

"I shall keep your guest occupied," Rory said, walking off in Clinton's direction.

"I watched your fiancé during dinner . . . and you must know he will never make you happy."

Marilyn frowned. How like Anna to make such an assumption based on what she saw. "I have every confidence in Stanley."

Making an unladylike snort, Anna slid her hand around Marilyn's elbow and urged her onto the verandah.

On the other side of the door, Anna turned, backing Marilyn against the wall, a hand on either side of her face. She leaned close, her breath warm against her cheek. "One night is all I ask. One night. Let me show you how wonderful it can be."

Marilyn glanced past her shoulder into the parlor. No one seemed to have noticed their sudden disappearance.

"Come with me. Just for a few minutes. I swear we won't be long."

"Where will we go?"

Anna didn't answer. She just took her by the hand and led her down the verandah steps and onto a stone pathway that was cast in darkness. Only a flickering lantern lit their way. "You are going to Claymoore Hall with your family?"

"Yes."

"I wish I could come."

Marilyn pressed her lips together. "Stanley wants me to stay in London."

"And do you want to stay in London . . . because of Stanley?"

Marilyn couldn't get the memory of Anna's touch out of her mind or the excitement that danced along her spine.

"I will rent a room at the Cavendish Hotel. I would very much like for you to come see me, Marilyn."

Marilyn licked her lips and Anna's gaze followed the path of her tongue.

"Please, come to me tomorrow."

"Marilyn!" It was Stanley.

"Good God, that man does not let you draw breath without him, does he? How very irksome."

"I must go."

Anna dropped Marilyn's hand and took a step away. "I'll be expecting you tomorrow, Marilyn."

Shannon slipped into Rory's room at twelve-thirty on the nose. He wasn't there.

All night she had paced her small room, terrified that Clinton would walk in at any moment and kill her.

How did he plan going about it? she wondered, hoping that Zach had remained out of sight. She prayed he did not harm Lord and Lady Graston's household because of them.

She would never forgive herself if that happened.

Walking across the room, she stared into the burning embers of the fire.

The door opened and closed, and Rory appeared. Her heart gave a leap. "Have you been waiting long?"

"No."

"Good." His gaze slid slowly down her body and back up again, and she wondered if he were able to see straight through her shift.

"Scandalous man," she said, as he lifted her up in his arms and slid her bottom onto a side table, settling between her thighs.

"The men in the room missed you when you left. One even commented on your absence."

Her heart missed a beat. "Oh, and who would that be?"

"Lady Anna's companion."

She swallowed past the lump in her throat. "I only wanted you to miss me."

He smiled against her lips. "You always know what to say."

She kissed his throat, his jaw, the lobe of his ear, and he moaned while he unbuttoned his trousers.

"You aren't going to undress?"

"I can't wait. I've wanted you all night."

His cock probed her entrance, and he slid inside her heat. Their mating was fast and furious. Shannon could sense his urgency, the need to claim her, and she clung to him, needing him, especially since she knew that soon she must leave him.

Their breaths mingled together as they met climax, and she said his name on a moan.

* * *

Anna was being so quiet.

Too quiet for Clinton's comfort level. He had hoped to get a glimpse of one of his cousins tonight, and he was stunned when Shannon had walked into the dining room. How far she had fallen in such a short time, and he could not help but remember the last night he had dined with her at the family estate in Dublin. She had worn a sapphire gown of the finest silk her mother had ordered from Paris, and her pale curls had been styled in a most pleasing manner, drawing more emphasis to her angelic features.

She was a prize, and well her family knew it.

And now she wore servants' garb and labored for her room and board.

Soon he would deal with his cousins but now he must put his friend at ease. Anna had watched him closely this past hour. She had said little as they'd stood awaiting the carriage and he'd been relieved by the silence, especially since he'd been busy looking frantically about for Zachary . . . but to no avail.

"Thank you for taking me tonight," Clinton said, sitting back against the velvet seat.

Anna stared at him but said nothing.

"You are angry."

"No, I am confused. You made a fool of me tonight in the way you stared at that servant."

He licked his lips, his mind racing. Anna might be young, but she was not stupid. "She looked familiar to me. I thought I remembered her from when she worked for another employer, but I was wrong."

"Why do I not believe you?"

His stomach tightened. He could not afford to fall from Anna's good graces. She was his ticket into the ton, and though she didn't have the best reputation, any reputation was better than none at all.

"I'd like to repay you in some way."

She lifted a brow.

Having seen evidence of her inhibition firsthand, he knew he had nothing to lose. He reached beneath her skirts, his fingers drifted up her calf, over her creamy smooth thighs, to her hot core.

"No drawers, Lady Anna. How very wicked you are."

Her legs opened and she glanced past his shoulders to the sheer, lace panels. She suddenly looked undecided. They had not yet moved, stuck in the line of carriages departing the estate.

He slid two fingers inside her and started pumping. She was so hot for him, so wet, and already he could imagine being balls deep inside her weeping core.

His thumb brushed over her clit and he added another finger. Her hips moved in time with his hand, and he continued stroking her faster and faster until she came, her honey drenching his fingers.

He went on his knees on the floor and settled between her spread thighs. She trembled, feeling his hot breath on her women's flesh. She nearly came off the seat when he licked her slit from back to front, lifting her clit with the tip of his tongue.

The carriage started to roll, and they passed by the front of the manor where a group of guests stood, awaiting their carriages. A shiver of excitement rolled through her. She had always enjoyed being watched while having sex. Had loved the parties where she had worn masks and wigs, leaving the guests guessing at identities. She knew people talked about her and the way she had been so lax with her charms, but she had given in to her excitement, to the moment, and now had to live with the consequences. Her grandmother had said she must change her reputation, but a reputation was a difficult thing to change, especially when she had done so much damage.

Those thoughts evaporated as Clinton's talented fingers squeezed her thighs and he probed her with his tongue.

His cock tented the front of his pants. He glanced up at her, and seeing where her gaze was riveted, unleashed his cock.

He pulled her bottom to the edge of the cushioned seat and slid into her with a moan.

The carriage slowed in traffic, and she had a moment of panic and could swear she heard a gasp. Her head fell back on her shoulders and she gripped the worn velvet seat as he thrust against her, over and over again.

It was so hot.

The heat was incredible, undeniable, and there was nothing Shannon could do to get away from it. Behind her eyelids she saw the bright light and heard the crackle and popping of wood in the distance.

A scream brought her awake, and she sat up in her bed abruptly.

The smoke was so thick she couldn't see her doorway because of it. The floorboards groaned beneath her and she came instantly alert.

The door opened and a figure appeared, his face covered in soot.

"Zachary?"

"Come on, Shannon. We have to get out."

"Where are Mum and Dad?"

"I don't know."

Panic the likes she'd never known rocked her. "We have to help them." she pleaded. But as they stepped out into the hall-

way, she saw the flames roaring up the stairwell. Her parents' chamber was on the first floor.

The heat was so intense, she could barely draw breath. And the smoke choked her lungs.

They rushed down the steps, and she could see the hallway was in flames. Her parents' chamber was at the opposite end of the hallway and she had no way of knowing if the flames had reached their wing yet.

"Fire!" she screamed from the top of her lungs, hoping that somehow her parents heard her, or better yet, had already made their way to safety.

Rory woke up out of a dead sleep, hearing the frantic call.

Shannon was beside him, her breathing uneven, and she let out a whimper.

The only light in the room came by way of the single candle that had burned down to a dim flame.

"Fire," she cried, and he lightly shook her.

She opened her eyes wide, looked at him, and blinked a few times.

"You were having a nightmare, Shannon."

Tears stained her face and he brushed them away with his thumbs.

His heart squeezed seeing the pain in her eyes, and he pulled her into his arms. "Come here."

She snuggled against his warmth.

His hand brushed up and down her back.

"What time is it?" she asked abruptly.

"I'm not sure."

She set up on her elbows and looked toward the clock on the mantel, but it was too dark to see the time. "You dreamt about a fire."

She stiffened but said nothing.

"Shannon, you need to trust me. I fear for you."

Her gaze dropped to his chest and he cursed beneath his breath.

"Do not be angry with me, Rory." Reaching up, she toyed with a lock of his hair. "I couldn't bear to have you mad."

She could get anything from him with those haunting blue eyes and that innocent smile. Indeed, he could not remember a time he had felt so strongly toward a lover. Fondness he had felt, and on occasion even a bit of possessiveness, but never an all-consuming need to make her his in every way.

"One day I shall tell you everything about my past."

He lifted her chin with his fingers and brushed his thumb over her full lower lip. "Do you promise?"

She nodded, "Yes, I swear."

21

Rory noted two things the following morning: His mother was angry with him, and Lady Kinkade was positively furious.

He understood the latter. He had heard Georgiana knock on his bedchamber door last night, but he had not answered. Thank goodness she had not lingered for too long.

But now he would have to explain the obvious. A locked door meant he didn't want her, but apparently she was not the type of woman to take no for an answer. Lord knows he had tried, and Lord knows she had tried, especially when she had taken him to the servants' party. He knew her intention. She wanted to make him jealous, or perhaps she had been out to prove a point. Whatever the case, it had backfired. He had become even more obsessed with Shannon, and he wanted her with everything he possessed.

And not just as a plaything. He had never been so intrigued, never so possessive, and this knowledge both frightened him and excited him.

Wishing Victor were awake and here to help, Rory piled his plate high with eggs, ham, and a scone, and made his way to his mother's side. Her gaze flicked over him; then she returned her attention to the newspaper.

She was not fooling him. She hated reading the newspaper, and had often mentioned how very depressing the news was. The only section that held any interest at all were the engagement and wedding announcements.

"A lovely soiree," Rory said to no one in particular.

His mother grunted and reached for her tea.

Lady Kinkade smiled tightly. "Indeed. Though I do wish you would have stayed up later, my lord."

"Yes, I was shocked you retired so early," his mother said. "It is unlike you to be among the first to leave the festivities."

"I am getting older, Mother."

"You were abed before one."

He didn't realize she had taken note of the precise hour.

"Perhaps you can make up for your absence by taking Lady Kinkade to Hyde Park today," his mother suggested.

The last thing he wanted was to leave the manor and Shannon, especially when so many questions remained unanswered. She had said she would tell him about her past, and he was ready to listen, but how could he do that if he wasn't around?

Lady Kinkade cleared her throat.

"Yes, of course," he replied, hoping he could talk Victor and Lillith into joining them.

The spark returned to Georgiana's eyes, and she smiled at him. Beneath the table, he felt her foot brush against his, her toes sliding up along his ankle and his shin.

God help him, it was going to be an extremely long day.

Shannon stood in Zachary's living quarters that set directly off the stables. The smell of leather, horses, hay, and manure was so strong it nearly took her breath away. "I wanted to make sure you were all right," she said, disturbed after last evening's vivid nightmare.

"I watched for Clinton last night, but I didn't see him." He tied a boot lace and then made busy retying the other. "We need to leave, Shannon. The risk is just too great if we stay."

She knew he spoke the truth, and yet she could not bring herself to make plans to leave. Although she didn't want to admit it, she had fallen desperately in love with Rory, and she had put her brother and herself in grave danger because of that love. "Where would we go?"

"What about Paris?"

"We don't speak fluent French." Actually, there had been a time she had thought living in France would be an appealing alternative, but now Paris seemed too far away.

"We know enough."

"No, not France."

He raked his hands through his hair. "You just don't want to leave your lover."

She flinched as though he'd struck her, and yet she didn't deny it.

"Did you tell him about Clinton?"

She shook her head. "No, of course not."

"Has he asked?"

"Yes, he saw Clinton staring at me last night. He knows something is amiss." She kept the part about the nightmare to herself, as well as her promise to tell Rory about their past.

She hated how torn she felt between Rory and her brother. Hated how guilt ate at her insides.

Tears burned the backs of her eyes. "I don't want to leave. I'm happy here."

"We have no choice, Shannon."

"I am tired of running."

He took a step closer to her. "Clinton has found us, Shannon. The man who killed our parents is closing in and he *will* kill us. It's only a matter of time."

Her heart pounded hard against her breastbone. "What if we go to Claymoore Hall with the family? From there we can go north, to Scotland."

His hold on her loosened and she saw his eyes light up. "We could not stay at Claymoore Hall long. Clinton will follow us."

"Maybe he won't."

"Shannon, he found his way into his lordship's dinner party. What is keeping him from having himself invited to their country manor?"

He made an excellent point.

The barn door opened and closed. "Zachary, are you here?" Shannon's breath caught in her throat. It was Rory.

"Stay here," Zachary whispered. "Yes, I'm here, my lord."

She nodded and sat down on his cot, fiddling with the rugged edge of the blanket. Last night she had heard Lady Kinkade knock at Rory's door. Shannon was not foolish enough to think the widow would give up. Rory was a prize worth fighting for.

Zachary had left the door slightly cracked, so she could still hear every word.

"What can I do for you, Lord Ambrose?"

"Could you prepare the phaeton for me?"

"Yes, my lord."

Shannon heard movement in the stable as her brother brought around the horses.

"Do you like London, Zachary?"

"Yes, sir."

Shannon glanced out the small window and could see Rory's strong back turned to her. Zachary was busy putting harnesses on the horses.

"I want you to know that if you and your sister need my assistance in any way, I am here to help you," Rory said, and Zachary glanced over at him.

"Thank you, my lord."

The two of them fell silent, and Shannon understood why when Georgiana appeared, dressed in a yellow muslin day dress with matching parasol. She was all smiles as she approached the two men.

"How lovely. A phaeton!"

She would enjoy being in an open carriage where everyone could see her with her beau.

Jealousy ate at Shannon's insides. Just last night she had made love to Rory with fevered abandon. It felt like they could never keep their hands off each other, and still, even with him courting another woman, she wanted him.

"Do not forget my offer," Rory said to Zachary as he helped Georgiana into the phaeton.

The other woman looked from one man to the other, but managed a smile. "Thank you for your assistance," she said prettily to Zach, who nodded and stepped back.

The phaeton pulled away, and only when they turned the corner out of the drive did he walk back to the stable.

Shannon met him at the door. "Perhaps we should tell him the truth. Maybe he can protect us."

Zach shook his head. "No, we won't involve anyone else in this. We will go to Claymoore Hall, and from there, we go to Scotland."

Anna stared out the window of her rented hotel suite at the wet streets below. Three hours had passed since the time Marilyn was supposed to meet her, and two hours ago a courier had arrived with a letter saying she would not make it, signed affectionately, M.

She had crumpled up the letter in her fist, tossed it into the fireplace, and then drank half a bottle of brandy before she sent word to Thomas.

She had seen Marilyn's face last night when they were out on the verandah. Could see how she trembled when they were close, the pulse in her throat beating wildly, their lips nearly touching. And yet she would deny her, and all for the overly fawning fiancé of hers. So what if he was a baron? He would keep Marilyn on a short leash, and that would not do at all.

Marilyn was too used to her freedom. Having a man like Stanley would be akin to having a controlling mother.

Below, in the street, she saw Thomas exit his newly purchased carriage and her heart picked up its pace. She opened the door and he swept off his hat. He was at her door minutes later. "I received your urgent summons. What is wrong?"

She felt slightly guilty that she had brought him here under the pretense of needing his assistance. "I was lonely."

Removing his gloves, he laid them on a nearby table and took a seat in a chair. "You, lonely? Now that is rich."

"I have also asked for a mutual friend to meet us here."

His lips curved. "Do tell me you speak of Lord Ambrose?"

Anna smiled. "That would be lovely, would it not? No, I fear Rory is occupied, but I do not think you will be disappointed."

"A pity. I did so enjoy our last encounter."

"Yes, well . . ."

He brushed a thumb over her chin. "Come, do not leave me guessing."

"The man I speak of is Clinton O'Connor, your fellow countryman."

His lips quirked. "Ah, yes, our recent companion with the mess of red hair and lovely lips."

"He likes you, I think," Anna said. "He's . . . curious."

"And I'm curious about him."

"There is a reason I am bringing him here, aside from the obvious, and you are going to help me."

He crossed his feet at the ankle and slouched in the chair. "What do you wish to know?"

"What he is after. Or rather, *who* he is after."

He frowned. "What gives you the impression he is after someone?"

"Call it a hunch."

"Your hunches usually prove to be correct."

In the weeks since the party at Claymoore Hall, they had formed a strong bond. True, that bond was based mostly on sex, but they were also friends, and Anna was growing to trust Thomas. They had gravitated toward each other, perhaps because they were so much alike.

"Well, what do you say?"

He removed his jacket and loosened his cravat. "I am only too happy to oblige. But what," he said, unbuttoning his trousers, "will you do for me?"

Clinton was greeted with quite a sight when he entered Lady Anna's hotel suite. Anna was on her knees between Thomas Lehman's spread thighs, and she was sucking his cock.

She was naked, save for sheer black stockings held up by silk garters, and with her blond hair falling down her back in thick waves, he could not help but think of his pretty little cousin.

He'd already smoked opium before coming over, the drug making him slightly light-headed and already he yearned for more.

"Would you like a drink?" Thomas asked, and Clinton nodded, helping himself from the side cupboard.

Thomas had a hand on Anna's shoulder, a gentle shove telling her that he'd had enough for now.

Understanding, Anna stood and walked toward Clinton, hips swaying. She was confident with her body, her waist small, her hips slightly curved, her mons completely bald. His fiancée would be horrified that a woman would do something so bold, but Clinton liked it, and found Anna and her sensual ways exciting.

Anna kissed him, sliding her tongue along the seam of his lips, seeking entry.

His gaze flicked from her to Thomas, and both watched him closely. "Drink up," she said, and he knocked back the entire glass in one swallow. Sex in the carriage had been exciting, but he had a feeling tonight would trump that experience.

She took him by the hand and motioned for Thomas to follow as she led them toward the large bed. She sat on the edge and spread her thighs wide.

Her hands moved up her belly to her breasts, where she started to play with her nipples, pulling on them. She made a tiny moan and bit her bottom lip with her top teeth.

Clinton could feel Thomas's gaze on him. "Make love to her," Thomas said, and it sounded like an order.

Clinton trembled with excitement as he removed his coat, waistcoat, and shirt.

He kissed Anna, then her breasts, working his way down her stomach to her sex. She was so hot, so wet, and when he licked her hot core, she groaned with delight just as she had last night.

She came quickly and instantly pulled him onto the bed and yanked off his trousers in record time.

She straddled his hips and slid herself onto his length a second later. "Lovely," she said with a soft smile. He cupped her small breasts. She glanced over at Thomas, and the other man climbed onto the bed and positioned himself behind her, and between Clinton's spread thighs.

Clinton felt Thomas slide his cock into her back passage, could feel the man's length against his own, separated only by the thinnest of tissue. With the other man seated fully inside her, she was impossibly tight. Anna leaned over Clinton, and Thomas over her.

Never in his life had he experienced anything so incredibly satisfying, and he was terrified he would finish before the other two.

He bit his lip, his hands fisting the sheets beneath him as they moved together as one.

22

The weather was horrible. Rain fell sideways, and the already heavily rutted roads became slick and impassable, making travel grueling, if not close to impossible.

It was with much relief when the party arrived at Claymoore Hall. Ironically, the moment the caravan rounded the final corner up the long drive, the rain stopped and a rainbow signaled that all would be right with the world.

However, Shannon felt anything but well as she followed Lady Graston to her quarters. The room was enormous and drafty. Though a fire had been lit, Shannon had a difficult time staying warm.

Any day now she would be leaving Claymoore Hall and Rory, and she would never see him again. She and Zachary had talked about it last night when the party had stopped overnight at an inn. He'd been adamant they not stay on at Claymoore Hall for long, and Shannon knew that he was right. Clinton would follow them. It was just a matter of time.

She could not risk her brother's life just because she was in love.

The thought of leaving Rory was excruciating. She had been avoiding him like crazy since the day he had taken Lady Kinkade into London. It hadn't helped that the widow had been showing off her lovely gold charm bracelet, a gift from Rory. Worse still, the single charm was in the shape of a heart.

If Shannon wasn't mistaken, Georgiana had smiled at her throughout dinner that evening, taunting her. How confident she was. Rory had done his best to get her attention, but Shannon would not glance at him even once.

Perhaps she behaved like a jealous wife, but she could not help it. He had made love to her, then turned around and bought another woman a trinket? It's not that she expected gifts from him. She didn't, and yet how easily he had given something to a woman he had admittedly told her he didn't care for.

"Are you well, my dear?" Lillith asked, and Shannon nodded, forcing a smile.

"Yes, of course. Just a little tired. I fear I did not sleep at all well last night."

"Forgive me for asking, but Rory is under the impression that you and your brother are in danger."

Her heart missed a beat. "I am not in danger, Lady Graston."

"If you were, you would tell me, though?"

"Of course."

Lillith watched her for a few unsettling moments, then nodded. "Very well, if you say you are fine, then I believe you. My brother-in-law seems to care for you both very much."

"I care for him as well."

She smiled. "Let him know how you feel, then. Show him, tell him. Don't let him wonder."

"I will. Thank you, Lady Graston."

"You're welcome." She placed a hand over her mouth and

yawned. "It has been a long, dreadful journey. Please retire for the evening and get a good night's rest. I shall see you in the morning."

"Good night, my lady."

Tears burned her eyes. She wanted to tell Rory she loved him, but she feared doing so. If he returned the sentiment, she would never leave him.

Shannon left the elaborate chamber and rushed down the hallway. The manor house was so large, it was easy to lose one's way.

Her chamber was on the ground floor and easily accessible to the kitchen. She stepped into the servant hallway and was met by Rory. "There you are."

"My lord," she said, dropping her gaze to his wide chest.

She could see his frown, sensed his disappointment at her reaction. "I have missed you, Shannon. Being stuck in that carriage for hours on end has only compiled my longing. I thought it would never end."

They had not made love for days, and her body ached for him. Even now, just being so close, her nipples hardened.

"Are you off for the night?"

"Yes."

"Come with me."

He took her by the hand and they walked down the servants' stairwell, which came to a hallway. He ducked his head out, and seeing the way clear, motioned for him to follow to his chamber.

Like Lord and Lady Graston's quarters, Rory's rooms were also incredible, with oversized mahogany furnishings and fabrics of bold browns and golds.

Setting before a fire was a bath, with steam rising off the surface.

She swallowed hard and looked away.

Already he was undressing, and try as she might, she could not help but stare at his beautiful body.

"Come, join me," he said, kicking off his shoes, and following with his stockings and then his trousers.

Her mouth went dry.

She didn't move.

He went to the bath, stepped in, and lowered his powerful body into the water. Her gaze focused on the high, tight ass, the thick, muscled thighs, the strong back, and broad shoulders.

Desire pulsing in every nerve, she undressed. He watched her in the cheval mirror, and she felt an odd sense of power as she slid out of the gown. The chemise clung to her body; she untied the ribbon that held it together and it fell to her feet.

She sat on a chair, slipped off her shoes, then slowly rolled down one stocking and then the other.

"Wait."

She glanced up at him.

"Spread your thighs."

She frowned but did as he asked, opening her thighs the slightest bit.

"More."

He made her feel positively wicked. Although she was embarrassed, she did as he asked and spread her legs wider, until each thigh slid over the sides of the chair.

"Let down your hair."

With trembling hands, she removed the clip that held her bun in place and the tresses came tumbling down.

"Yes, that's nice. Now play with your breasts."

She licked her lips and lifted her hands to her breasts. The nipples stabbed into her palms and tightened into tiny buds. A rush of excitement touched her spine as she cupped the small mounds and then, using her fingers, touched the rigid peaks.

He released a moan and shifted in the tub.

Sensing his excitement, she continued to play with herself, rolling her nipples between her fingers and thumbs, and pulling, much as he would do when pleasuring her. A sharp ache began to grow between her thighs, and she slid one hand down her stomach, through the nest of tight curls that covered her sex.

"Yes," Rory said from the tub.

She was already wet. Her flesh was sensitive, and as her fingers rolled over the tight bud at the top of her sex, she bit her bottom lip.

Rory had never seen anything as sexy as Shannon pleasuring herself. This was a woman who had been a virgin not so very long ago, and watching her touching herself was extremely gratifying. Already he was as hard as stone.

She pulled at her nipple while sliding a finger inside her sweet, tight quim. He could see the moisture there, and it was his undoing.

"Come here, Shannon." His voice was husky.

She licked her lips again, and he anticipated those soft pillows wrapped around his cock.

Doing as he asked, she walked across the room, and he didn't take his eyes off her. She had never been so excited in all her life.

"Sit on the edge of the tub," he demanded, nodding toward the opposite side.

She sat down, easing her legs open as she gripped the edge tight.

His gaze shifted from hers, to her breasts, to her sex. She could see his cock in the clear water, the way it reared against his belly.

Then he was between her thighs, spreading them wide, his breath hot against her woman's flesh.

His tongue barely grazed her and she cried out in ecstasy. He stroked her from back passage to clit, teasing the tiny nub with the tip of his tongue.

"Get into the tub, turn around, on your knees."

She did as he said, turning her back to him and going up on her knees, her fingers gripping the sides of the bathtub.

Once again he tasted her, his finger toying with her clit. With his free hand he reached beneath her and cupped her breast, teasing a nipple.

He slid his cock into her and she sucked in a breath. He moved slowly, his strokes long and even.

Rory clenched his jaw. She was so tight, so wet. He cupped her breasts, teasing the nipples, her sighs and moans telling him she was getting closer to orgasm by the second.

Shannon cried out as she met climax, and Rory followed behind with a guttural moan.

With trembling legs, she eased back into the tub and the warm water. Rory slid his hands around her, hugging her to him, and she relaxed against his wide chest as he kissed her neck and shoulder.

She could get used to such moments, the intimacy one could share with another. If only they could have such a future.

"I am glad you came to Claymoore Hall. There are so many things I want to show you."

She smiled, content and sated. "Did you spend a lot of time here as a child?"

"I did. My mother has always preferred the country to the city. My brothers and I would run wild and free. There was always so much to do."

She had also been brought up in a large manor house on acreage. She had always loved horses. One of the most difficult parts about being in servitude was that she never had time to herself, and never was able to ride. At least Zachary had been more fortunate.

"Perhaps tomorrow I can talk Lillith into giving you time off."

"The other servants will be angry with me," she said, glancing back at him. "There are already some who believe I have been given too much for the short amount of time I have worked for Lady Graston, and I do not blame them. I should not receive special privledges."

He brushed a curl over her ear. "Shannon, what if when we returned to London, I set you up in your own apartment?"

Understanding the question fully, she looked away. Disappointment ate at her insides. He wanted her as his mistress, not his wife. What did she expect? She was a servant, after all. Too far beneath him to marry.

She took a deep breath, released it. "You wish me to be your mistress?"

"I do." He placed a kiss on her shoulder. "I'll take care of you, Shannon. You will never have to work again."

Yes, but for how long? Until he tired of her and replaced her with another? It didn't matter anyways. She was leaving in a couple of days and she would never see him.

"My brother—"

"I would never separate you. He can live in your household. Whatever will set your mind at ease, I shall do."

"Let me think on it," she said, hoping the answer appeased him.

"I'll treat you well, Shannon. You'll never have to worry about struggling again. I'll protect you. I won't let anyone harm you in any way."

The declaration made her throat tighten. For a moment, she

allowed herself the luxury of dreaming about what her life could be like. What it would feel like to be with Rory and under his protection.

As lovely as that fantasy was, she realized she wanted more. She didn't want to be just his mistress . . . she wanted to be his wife.

23

Lady Anna could not recall ever darkening the door of a library, and yet she felt compelled to do just that after her disturbing conversation with Clinton O'Connor.

Last night he had once again drank a lot of whiskey and smoked opium, the combination effectively loosening his tongue. When he started slurring his words, she had asked specific questions, being careful to skirt the issue of Shannon and Zachary. He had made mention of a fire, that he would inherit a fortune and then all those who had denied him would come crawling to him.

"May I help you, my lady?"

Lady Anna smiled at the buxom lady before her, glasses perched on the end of her nose. "Yes, I believe so . . . I am looking for information about a fire that might have taken place in Dublin earlier this year."

"I shall see what I can do." The librarian disappeared in a back room for a quarter of an hour, then resurfaced with a substantial stack of papers and set them on a table. "The publication comes out every week. If it is newsworthy, it would be here."

Anna looked at the heap with growing dismay. Perhaps she should have asked Thomas for assistance, but he was no doubt sleeping the day away.

"You may want to wear gloves, so as not to get ink on that lovely dress of yours."

"I shall, thank you," Anna murmured.

"Let me know if I can help you in any way," the lady said, walking toward her desk, where a large stack of books awaited her.

An hour later, Anna was quickly losing hope of finding any information that would be helpful, and the kink in her neck was not helping her foul mood one bit.

She set the newspaper on the stack of those she'd scoured, and her heart lurched seeing the heading: PROMINENT DUBLIN BUSINESSMAN AND FAMILY PERISH IN DEADLY FIRE.

Her hands began shaking when the name O'Connor jumped from the pages. Earl, Ennis, and their children, daughter Shannon, and son Zachary, all died in the blaze, it said.

Her stomach twisted sickeningly as she realized the possibility that she had been cavorting with the O'Connors' killer. From what the newspaper said, Clinton was the only living heir, and he had been hunting the night of the fire with another servant. Anna wondered how he had come to know that Shannon and Zachary had escaped the blaze.

"How are you doing?"

Anna jumped when the librarian appeared from behind her.

She glanced at the paper. "You found what you were looking for?"

"Yes, I'm wondering if you have pen and paper. I need to write down information."

"Of course."

Bringing the items Anna asked for, the librarian rushed off to help another patron.

Anna could barely keep her hand steady as she wrote. She must tell Rory of her findings immediately.

Marilyn had just fallen asleep when she woke to someone pounding at the door.

Her aunt and Lord Graston had left for Claymoore Hall, and the manor felt extremely empty without them. Now she wished that she had gone, but she had stayed in London because Stanley had asked her to stay.

Since a skeleton crew had been left behind, Marilyn went to the front door and opened it. "Lady Anna."

"Did Shannon and Zachary leave town with your aunt and Lord Graston?"

She looked so pale, so concerned, that Marilyn became frightened. "Yes, why?"

"May I come in?"

Marilyn led her into the parlor where she'd been reading. Anna shut the door behind them. "I fear that Shannon and Zachary are in grave danger. I have discovered that their cousin was responsible for setting fire to their family home in Ireland."

"What on earth?"

"Apparently he meant to kill the entire family, but Zachary and Shannon escaped."

"How do you know this?" Marilyn asked, looking alarmed.

"The man I brought to Lord and Lady Graston's party, Clinton O'Connor, he is Shannon's cousin."

"Oh God," Marilyn said. "I thought Shannon was acting rather strangely the night of the soiree. She seemed taken aback upon seeing Clinton." She brushed a hand over her face. "I do not know what to do."

"We must warn them. I do not want to just send a letter."
Marilyn shook her head. "No, we must go there."
Anna's brow furrowed. "We?"
"Yes, I will go with you."
"Go home, pack, and I shall meet you in an hour."

Shannon glanced toward where her horse grazed in the meadow. The white gelding that had looked so demure had a wildness about her that she related to. When she had left the stable, she had felt Zachary watch her. He had not at all been happy when she told him she was going for a ride alone. In fact, he'd insisted on going with her . . . until she confessed she was meeting Lord Ambrose.

She had seen the disappointment in his eyes, and the concern. But she wouldn't let that stop her from meeting up with Rory.

Again, she could not help but think of the question he'd asked her. How tempting it was to agree to become his mistress. Lord knows her life would be much easier than it was now if she were to accept, and she could think of nowhere else she would rather be, or who she'd like to be with, than with him.

And yet she had to remember where she came from, and that women who became mistresses were asking for a lifetime of unhappiness. One day Rory would marry, and she would be the other woman, waiting patiently for him to come to her. And what if she was with child? That child would be a bastard and never recognized as a true heir, but instead joining the ranks of yet another blueblood's by-blow.

She heard hoofbeats headed her way and could not help the excitement that rushed through her at seeing Rory in the distance, coming toward her.

He wore brown leather breeches tucked into a pair of well-worn knee-high boots and a linen shirt, open at the neck. His long hair was ruffled from the breeze, and as he dismounted, an ache grew deep inside her heart.

Lord help her, but she loved him.

Desperately.

Desire was a dangerous thing, she knew that, and yet as he came toward her, arms open wide, she knew that she could never tell him no. He could tell her he was the devil and it would not matter.

He swung her around, her legs coming up off the ground, and she smiled as his laughter vibrated through her.

His arms held her tight, and with hands on his shoulders, she looked up at the sun and blue sky, and was unable to remember a time she had been so happy.

The ends of his dark hair tickled her fingers, and as he set her back on her feet, he leaned in and kissed her.

It was a gentle kiss, a light pressure against her lips. "I have a surprise for you."

"A surprise?"

"Yes, we'll have to ride a little ways."

She started toward her mount, but he shook his head. "I want you to ride with me. I need to feel you in my arms."

Exhilaration danced along her spine. The words pleased her in every way. He helped her mount the beautiful black thoroughbred and slipped behind her, pulling her close against his chest. She relaxed completely, and as they started across the meadow, she smiled to herself, content to forget about everything else and just enjoy the moment.

The village was tiny and had an impressive market. The atmosphere was exhilarating, with an old man playing the fiddle and young children dancing on the green lawns. A girl close to Shannon's age sold flowers, and she seemed intrigued by Rory, as were all the people in the village. Shannon felt a sudden surge of pride that she was with him, walking hand in hand, looking at the wares. She saw the envy in the women's eyes, and when Rory bought her a simple silver locket, she was on top of the world.

"Thank you," she said, rubbing the cherished necklace between thumb and forefinger, trying without success to forget the bracelet he'd bought for Georgiana.

"You deserve to be spoiled, Shannon."

She felt a blush rush up her neck as he watched her with a familiar gleam in his eye.

"I want to spoil you, and I hope for that opportunity."

Meaning he wanted her as his mistress.

A girl who could not be five years old tugged on Shannon's skirts. "Flowers?" she asked, her vibrant green eyes hopeful, her cheeks like two tiny apples. Braids bracketed her cherub-like face, and when she smiled, Shannon's heart melted.

Rory reached into his pocket and pulled out a coin, much more than the flowers cost, and pressed it into her chubby hand. "Thank you, love."

The girl beamed at Rory, and Shannon's heart warmed toward him even more. He handed Shannon the small bouquet of wild flowers.

The rest of the afternoon was a dream, and when they returned to Claymoore Hall, Shannon was on top of the world. Zachary had said nothing to her when they entered the stables, but she could see the disappointment in his eyes. She would not let her brother's disapproval ruin the exhilaration she felt.

She was right on Rory's heels when her brother cleared his throat. She turned and glanced at him, as did Rory.

He looked right at the locket, a strange expression on his face. Was that disappointment?

"Thank you," she replied, and followed Rory out the door.

He dropped her hand immediately and knew they would have to part ways before anyone in the manor saw them.

"Come to me tonight?" he asked.

"I shall try."

She could tell he wanted to kiss her, but he wouldn't. Not here where they ran the risk of someone seeing them. In fact, he had only kissed her once today. He had surprised her when they had not stopped to make love. Her body had burned for him, and she had felt the evidence of his desire against her back when they had ridden.

And despite the fact she wanted him, the waiting would make it all the sweeter.

Hiding the bouquet in her skirts, she rushed into the room, put the flowers in a glass of water, and lay down on the mattress, reliving every second of the afternoon they had shared.

He had made no mention of her past, but he had asked her about herself, what she enjoyed doing, her favorite color, her favorite book, her favorite artist.

And he had been surprised by some of her responses . . . in a good way, if the smile on his lips were to tell.

Exhausted from lack of sleep these past nights, she closed her eyes and dreamt of Rory.

24

Shannon could feel her brother's gaze on her as she followed the other servants across the green lawns of Claymoore Hall. She struggled with the weight of the basket she held, and Johnny had already tried to carry it for her, but she waved him off.

Was it her imagination, or did everyone know about her little excursion into town with Rory?

This morning when she'd walked into the kitchen, the other servants went silent. The sidelong stares and quirked lips made her realize she had been seen with Lord Ambrose.

Shannon set the basket down and helped another of the servants lay out blankets. Lady Rochester and her entourage were walking across the grass toward them, and Shannon's stomach tightened upon seeing Rory. He walked beside his brother, laughing at something Victor said.

"A handsome sight, aren't they?" a nearby middle-aged servant said, and Shannon nodded.

Georgiana walked with the group, and Shannon felt a spike of jealousy race through her. What a happy family they made.

By the time the group descended upon the picnic, the servants had blended into the background, some returning to the manor to finish their duties, while others, like herself, had to stand aside in case her mistress or master needed her.

Georgiana sat beside Rory, so close their legs touched. She even kicked off her shoes. She nibbled on fruit, cheese, and bread, and drank enough wine to become giddy.

Shannon unconsciously rubbed the locket that was hidden beneath the high bodice of her gown, nestled against her heart. At Claymoore Hall she was able to wear her own clothes and do away with the gray uniform that had been required at Lord and Lady Graston's estate. Though she wore one of her favorite gowns, it paled in comparison to Georgiana's, which accented the woman's best features.

Lady Graston required little attention, and Shannon had a moment where she almost returned to the manor, but she did not want speculation to run rampant. It was difficult to sit and pretend indifference when the man she loved was flirting with the woman he would no doubt marry.

"Ye are far mare beautiful than she," a voice said in her ear, and she nearly jumped out of her skin. She had not even seen Johnny approach.

She didn't embarrass herself by asking him what he meant by his comment, especially when her jealousy was obviously apparent to everyone around her. "You are too kind."

"I tell the truth."

She met his gaze and smiled. He was such a nice young man, and any girl would be lucky to gain his favor.

"Just be careful, Shannon. I do not want to see ye get hurt."

Although she knew he was well meaning, the words were like a stake to the heart. "I appreciate your concern, Johnny."

"If ye ever need someone to talk to, please know I am always here."

"Thank you, Johnny," Shannon said, feeling Rory's gaze on her.

"Lord Ambrose, will you take me for a walk?" Georgiana asked in a too-sweet voice, loud enough for Shannon to hear.

Rory looked like he would rather do anything else. "Of course he will," Lady Rochester said from where she sat nearby.

His dark hair was held back in a queue, drawing more emphasis to his handsome face, and Shannon could see the nerve in his jaw twitch. "As my mother is so gracious to point out, yes, I would be happy to take you on a walk."

"I would not want to force you." Georgiana flashed a cool smile.

Standing, Rory reached out a hand. "Come, Lady Kinkade. Let us enjoy this lovely afternoon." Georgiana slid her fingers around his and came to her feet.

As the two walked off, arm in arm, Shannon tried not to let her gaze linger on Rory's impressive backside.

Yesterday, when she had fallen asleep, she had slept right through the night and woke at dawn. She knew Rory would wonder where she had been.

Her bedmate had been awake, reading a book, and she had grunted a greeting as Shannon readied herself for the day. Now she wished she had taken more care in her appearance because she felt like she paled in comparison to Georgiana in every way.

It didn't help that the two made a handsome couple, well-suited in all ways, and they would be the toast of the ton.

She caught her brother's gaze, and his brow lifted as though to say, "How can ye be so bloody foolish, Shannon?"

Georgiana's laughter made her clench her teeth.

If Shannon became Rory's mistress, this would be her life—waiting for him to come to her when he wasn't with his family.

"You deserve better," Johnny murmured under his breath, before walking off in the opposite direction.

* * *

Clinton watched the small group walk across the green lawns of Claymoore Hall from where he stood hidden in the thick foliage.

The Georgian manor was impressive, if not a bit pretentious with its massive fountains that included Neptune rising from the waters. Gwendolyn had said she wanted such a feature at their Dublin estate, and maybe he would appease her, if only to help to alleviate some of the guilt he felt in recent days.

His time in London had not been all about business. Lady Anna and Thomas Lehman had initiated him into a lifestyle he had never before considered, and he had a difficult time telling them no. In fact, he'd spent the entire night at the hotel with them, smoking opium, drinking whiskey, and having sex.

All night long.

His face flushed at the memories of all they had done, at the wicked things he had allowed them both to do, and what he had done in turn.

Even now he knew he would look them up one last time before he returned to Ireland. And the sooner he finished his business here, the sooner he could make one final visit to the duo. First, he just had to figure out a way to get to his young cousins.

Fortunately, getting inside the sprawling manor would be easier than the Twickenham estate, but the challenge here was getting in and out without anyone seeing him.

He had been half-tempted to ask Jacob to come with him to finish the job he had started, but during their last meeting he had seen suspicion in the other man's eyes. He said he was returning to Dublin, and perhaps it was out of his own guilt, but he told the private investigator to keep an eye on Gwendolyn until he returned.

As the youngest Rayborne brother approached with the beautiful redhead on his arm, Clinton slinked into the brush. Time was of the essence. He needed to make his move soon. Get in, get out, and then he would never look back. He would return to London for a short sojourn to experience more of what Anna and Thomas had to offer, to once again smoke the drug that had a calming quality about it, to feel their hands on his body. For a few hours he could forget about everything: his dark past, the murders of his aunt and uncle, his infuriating cousins, and most of all, the knowledge that one missed step could cause his entire world to crumble around him like a house of cards.

Lord and Lady Mawbry's arrival was met with great ceremony. The finest china and most ornate silver was brought out, and the most delicate of lace tablecloths graced the tables. Rory was thrilled to see Sinjin, his eldest brother again, who had already given him a lecture on the risks of dueling and went on to say how very fortunate he was to be alive.

Seeing her son and his wife, Betsy beamed like a young girl as she stared at Sinjin and Katelyn from across the grand table.

"We have missed you ever so much. How are you feeling, my dearest?" Lady Rochester asked Katelyn, Lady Mawbry, who was pregnant with Betsy's first grandchild.

"I am well, thank you, Lady Rochester."

Sinjin took a sip of his brandy and set it down. "Do not let her fool you, Mother. She has been sick for weeks now."

"No!" Betsy said, setting down her glass none too gently.

"I fear he is right," Katelyn said with a reassuring smile. "I felt queasy most of the way to Claymoore Hall."

"Well, let me assure you that it is probably just in passing." Lady Rochester pressed a napkin to her lips "I was very ill with Sinjin as well."

"Little wonder," Victor murmured, a teasing grin on his lips.

It was wonderful for Rory to be in the company of his family, especially Sinjin, who he had missed desperately these past weeks. His brother looked incredibly happy, much like Victor and Lillith. Would he ever know that happiness, he wondered? In the times they had been together he had caught but a glimmer of what life could be like. But his brothers had both married for love.

He was not a greedy man, but he wished in this that he had a choice. That his rank and title would not require him to marry amongst the titled and privileged. His mother would never allow for him to marry a servant. He knew that, especially now that she had welcomed Lady Kinkade into the family. To bring his father to Claymoore Hall to meet Georgiana was saying that she felt the deed was already done.

"Well, how about the women join me in the parlor for tea and the men can go out for cigars."

"Hear, hear," Victor said, already standing.

Rory glanced toward the door that led to the kitchen. He was starving for the sight of Shannon, and as the days went on, with all of his family in attendance, time alone would be rare indeed. He could only hope to see her when they did things as a family, like earlier at the picnic, and she had barely glanced at him, though he had felt her eyes on him as he'd walked with Lady Kinkade.

He hated hurting her at all, but how could it be helped when his mother had been so determined to bring Georgiana along?

Rory followed his brother out onto the verandah. Sinjin put an arm around his shoulder. "How has my little brother been?"

"I am well."

His gaze shifted to Rory's shoulder. "How is the wound?"

"Healing."

"I understand you have stayed out of trouble since your last duel?"

"Yes, but only because he has found someone to keep him occupied," Victor added.

"Lady Kinkade, I presume."

Victor's lips quirked, and he brought the cigar to his lips and inhaled deeply, blowing the smoke out above his head.

"Georgiana is lovely," Rory remarked.

"But you don't want her," Sinjin said, his eyes narrowing, a smile playing at his lips. "You forget I know you too well, brother."

"Yes, you do. And you're right. I don't want her."

"But Mother is under the impression you will be asking for her hand."

Victor snorted.

Rory chewed on his thumbnail. "She is wrong."

"You want someone else?" Sinjin asked, his gaze shifting to Victor for a moment before settling on Rory once again.

"I do."

Sinjin rested a hip against the stone wall. "Well, do not keep me in suspense any longer. Who is this mysterious other woman?"

Shifting on his feet, Rory blurted, "Have you seen Lily's maid? The one with the pale blond hair and blue eyes."

"She was with Lillith when we arrived, correct?" Sinjin asked, his brows furrowing, and Rory could already sense his disapproval.

"Yes, she is the one," Rory said matter-of-factly, ready to defend the woman he loved.

"She's beautiful." Sinjin sounded jovial enough, but Rory could hear the hesitation in his voice.

"She isn't like most servants, Sin."

Sinjin laughed under his breath and Rory felt his cheeks flush. "She may not be like other servants, but the point is she is a servant, Rory. Mother would never agree to such an arrangement."

"I love her."

Victor's mouth formed an O, while Sinjin's brows rose.

"And I want to marry her."

"She is a servant," Sinjin said again, crossing his arms over his chest. "You cannot marry her."

"Why? You married a woman below your station."

"Yes, but you must remember that Katelyn's father was an earl."

"An earl who had gambled away his fortune."

Sinjin smiled sympathetically. "True, but he was still an earl, Rory. Do not get me wrong, I want you to be happy. I just know that Mother will not allow you to marry this servant."

"Her name is Shannon."

Victor cleared his throat and looked more than a little out of sorts. He had not said anything yet, but he looked like he wanted to.

Rory brushed a hand through his hair. "I want her."

"Then make her your mistress," Sinjin urged.

"I already asked her."

"And she refused?" Victor replied, sounding surprised.

"No, but she didn't accept either. She just hasn't answered me." And she had not bothered to come to his room last night. He had thought their afternoon alone together would have brought them closer, and he had wanted to ask her what her decision was, but he'd been hesitant to ask her, fearful of her answer.

"Her brother works for us as well," Victor said to Sinjin. "Perhaps she is worried about her future."

"I don't think that is it, because I offered Zachary a position." Rory kneaded the tense muscles at the base of his neck.

"She must be content in Victor's household if she did not accept."

Rory didn't know that either. "I think she is in trouble. Actually, I think both she and her brother are in trouble."

"Rory believes she is not being honest about her identity, and I admit that not everything adds up," Victor said.

"Perhaps it is time to get to the bottom of the matter then?" Sinjin said matter-of-factly.

Rory knew Sinjin was right. "I have asked her specific questions about her past, and the brother as well, but neither of them are forthcoming."

Sinjin shrugged. "Then maybe you are worrying for nothing."

"Perhaps," Rory said, his heart leaping when he caught sight of Shannon through the large windows. She was handing a shawl to Lillith, and Lillith was introducing her to Katelyn.

He knew in his heart that the three would get along famously, and that together they could all be one happy family.

Shannon nodded at something Katelyn said, and Georgiana leaned in closer; Shannon's smile faded before she walked off.

"I must go," Rory said, leaving his brothers.

"Where are you off to?" Victor asked.

Rory smiled. "To talk to my future wife."

25

Shannon liked Katelyn very much. She envied the woman, who was so obviously in love with her husband and expecting their first child. What must it feel like to be married to the man of your dreams and be carrying his child?

"Be a dear and get me another glass of wine, will you?" Georgiana had asked Shannon in a too-sweet voice. She wasn't fooled one bit. The other woman despised her and used every opportunity to prove it.

"Of course, my lady," she replied, and went into the parlor where the liquor was kept to pour a drink. She took a steadying breath and reached for a wineglass in the cabinet.

Rory walked in and she very nearly dropped the glass.

"Where were you last night?" he asked softly, the backs of his fingers brushing along her jaw. His touch was heaven, and she wanted to throw herself into his arms but did not dare for fear of someone walking in on them.

"I fell asleep after we returned from town, and I did not wake until this morning. I am sorry."

Was she mistaken, or was that relief shining in his eyes? "I worried that maybe I said something wrong."

"No," she replied, her heart missing a beat when his thumb brushed over her lower lip.

"You are not wearing the locket?" His voice hinted at disappointment.

"Here," she said, touching the slender locket that rested against her heart.

His hand covered hers, his fingers grazing the slope of her breasts.

Another servant walked in and stopped short seeing them.

Rory removed his hand, but it was too late. The footman had clearly seen them, the slight quirk of his lips saying he had noted where Rory's hand had been. Rumors would be circulating throughout the servants' quarters, and Zachary would be furious.

Of course, the servants were already talking. She had expected as much when she went riding with Rory. Though they had tried to go unnoticed, word would spread and soon everyone would know about them.

She reached past Rory, grabbed the bottle of wine from the shelf, and poured a liberal amount into the glass. "I must return."

"Come to me tonight?"

She wanted to be alone with him more than anything, but she was afraid of risking it. "I have to wait until my roommate falls asleep."

"I will see if you can get your own room."

"No, people are already talking."

She had thought the news that others were talking about them might startle him, but he seemed not at all bothered. "Very well."

Midnight was only an hour away, and she wanted to see him

again, to spend one more night in his arms, to make love to him and memorize his features for all the lonely nights ahead of her.

She hoped that once she left, he would never forgot her . . . because she would never forget him.

He kissed her, and she smiled against his lips before turning back to the cabinet. "What did Georgiana say to you?"

"She asked for a drink."

"She doesn't like you. She knows I have feelings for you."

Feelings. Not love, but feelings. The problem was she was in love with Rory. Helplessly in love.

Not wanting him to see her disappointment, she said, "I must go now. I shall see you tonight if I can."

Shannon walked into Rory's chamber.

The room was so dark she could barely see her hand in front of her face, the only light a flickering candle that cast shadows upon the fine silk wallpaper.

Naked to the waist, Rory stood by the fire, one arm resting on the heavy mantel. Seeing her, he smiled. "I was wondering if you would come."

It was one in the morning. She had yearned to come earlier, but it had been difficult to get past Greta, the servant she had been paired with to share a room. Thank goodness the woman slept like the dead, but she always read, and tonight of all nights, she had been exceedingly engrossed in her novel. "I am sorry I'm late."

His teeth flashed in the darkened room. "I am just glad you were able to make it."

She went to him and he embraced her, his strong arms pulling her close. Tears burned the backs of her eyes and she pressed a kiss to his chest, to the wound that had healed so well.

She kissed his neck, his shoulder, and slowly went to her knees on the rug. He unbuttoned his trousers, and she released his thick cock, sliding her mouth over the impressive crown. She weighed the heavy sac in her hand, while running a hand up and down the velvety shaft. He went to his knees and kissed her, his cock rearing up against her belly. Slowly he eased her onto her back. His long hair fell away from his face, brushing against her breasts as he leaned down to kiss a nipple, his tongue sliding around the delicate bud.

Fire rushed through her veins, sending a pulsing ache between her thighs, where his hips lay, his huge cock pressed snug against her.

She watched him pleasure her, enjoyed the way his long lashes cast shadows on his high cheekbones. It was exhilarating. As he slipped down her belly, excitement rolled along her spine.

Never would she forget this moment, or the way he made her feel. He was a lover unlike any she would ever have. Lady Kinkade would no doubt get to call him husband, and Shannon would be jealous of her for all eternity.

He licked her slit over and over again, stroking her clit with his long tongue.

He slid his cock inside her snug entrance and groaned as she tightened around him. Her thighs fell open and her nails grazed his back, sliding down over his buttocks, her fingers clenching him, urging him to thrust harder and deeper.

They came together with heated moans, their kiss deep and passionate.

The door closed and he looked up, but not in time to see who it had been. He hadn't heard the door open, and he didn't want to alert Shannon that someone had seen them. His pants were shoved down around his knees, and Shannon's chemise rode past her waist, her breasts totally exposed. And with her platinum blond hair, no one would wonder who his lover was. They would know, and the household would be talking come tomorrow.

"What is it?" she asked, glancing toward the door.

"Nothing. I just heard someone walk past."

"You don't think they heard us, do you?"

"Doubtful," he said, loving the desire in her eyes, the flushed cheeks and sated expression.

She nodded and released a sigh. "I cannot stay long."

"Please for a little while."

He didn't want to move from where they lay on the rug, their bare limbs intertwined.

Georgiana's nails bit into her palms.

Damn that little bitch.

Her maid had told her that Lord Ambrose and Shannon were seen in town yesterday. Today she had watched Rory as the pretty servant talked to the handsome footman named Johnny. He'd tried not to show his irritation or how distracted he was, but his jealousy had been obvious.

And now she heard the two making love . . . again. She had come to Rory's room hoping to seduce him, to win him over, especially since he had polished off a bottle of wine during their game of chess.

She had been able to capture his attention during that short time, and only because Shannon had left the room. The man panted after her like a dog in heat. Did he not realize he was making a fool of himself and of her as well? Why did men constantly think with their cocks rather than with their heads?

All evening she'd considered having a conversation with Lady Graston about Shannon. Perhaps the other woman would send Shannon back to her Twickenham estate while the family spent these weeks at Claymoore Hall. Once Georgiana had the engagement ring on her finger, she would not allow Rory to go anywhere near his brother's estate, and she would keep him on a very tight leash. She would never tolerate other women throwing themselves at her husband.

But even Lady Graston seemed to dote on the girl, singing her praises, saying how fortunate she was that Lord Graston had found her.

Shannon would no doubt forever be a thorn in Georgiana's side.

Honestly, if it wasn't for the fact that Lady Rochester seemed to like her, Georgiana might pack her bags and return to London to pursue another man. She wasn't getting any younger, and she wanted the protection of marriage once again. Although Rory hardly had the title she had desired, he made up for it in every other way.

She could hardy wait to make love to him, to experience ecstasy in his arms. She had eagerly lapped up all the stories, seen the gleam in his lovers' eyes as they whispered under their breath about being taken by the dangerous rakehell.

She wanted to be taken in such a way—roughly, desperately, like he couldn't wait another second to have her.

Unfortunately, as it was now, he locked his door against her every night. But he didn't lock that little slut out.

Feeling like a knife had been shoved into her chest, Georgiana walked back to her chamber, an idea forming in her mind.

Desperate times called for desperate measures.

26

"Shannon, we must leave now . . . while the family is out."

Shannon's stomach dropped to her toes. "Now? But it's mid-afternoon."

Zachary brushed a hand through his hair. "The family went to the abbey for the day. From what the other servants said, the abbey is five miles away from the manor."

Shannon was aware the family and guests had gone for a walk. Lady Graston had not asked Shannon along, and though she yearned to go, especially since Rory would be there, she had instead watched the progression as they walked across the lawns, Georgiana clinging to Rory's arm.

Last night when Rory had fallen asleep in Shannon's arms, she had stared at him, memorizing his features, knowing that that moment would have to suffice for all the days ahead when she would miss him so very much.

"We cannot wait until tomorrow?"

"Shannon, we have the perfect opportunity, and this way we'll have plenty of sunlight left in which to travel. I have two horses we can use."

"No."

"What do you mean no?"

"We will not steal from them. Lord and Lady Graston have been too kind to us, and we will not return the favor by taking their family's horses."

"They would understand. We can leave a note."

"And say what, exactly?"

Zach shrugged. "That it was a matter of emergency that we took them. That we will pay them back one day."

"No, I refuse to do that."

He sighed heavily and ran a hand through his hair. "It will take us far too long on foot."

"I don't care."

"Fine." He stared at her, his frustration obvious.

"Meet me at the back gate in five minutes."

Shannon nodded and rushed to her chamber and packed her few things. Tears clogged her throat knowing she would never again see the man she loved more than life. Perhaps she should write a letter and leave it for him where he would find it eventually. At least then Rory would know leaving had nothing to do with him.

But time would not allow it. Zachary was waiting.

The day dragged on endlessly.

Rory walked the grounds of the abbey with Georgiana, trying with difficulty to focus on what she was saying. It was not easy when his thoughts were with a pretty blonde servant who had been left back at the manor house.

He wanted to ask Lillith where Shannon was or why she hadn't been asked along, but he knew the answer when he saw Georgiana and noted the tight smile on her face when he'd entered the parlor. He'd awoken late and completely missed breakfast. For all that he tried not to know what her expression meant, he knew very well that she had been the one to walk in on them last night. And there was nothing he could do or say to defend himself.

Plus, he had half a mind not to defend himself. Georgiana was here at his mother's invitation, not his own, and the sooner she realized they would not have a future together, the better.

He was relieved when the others gathered up their things and started walking back toward the manor house.

Thank God.

"I was thinking that perhaps we could take a day or two to journey to York," Georgiana said. "I have heard so much about the medieval village and castle."

Though he always enjoyed visiting York, he had no desire to leave Claymoore Hall—or Shannon.

"My father is soon to arrive, and I need to be here."

"Oh yes, that's right," she said, pressing her lips together. "Of course. How thoughtless of me to think otherwise. I am sure you miss him terribly."

"Indeed, I do." He was more than anxious to speak with his father, because he wanted his approval to marry Shannon. Lord Rochester was a man of few words, and he had little patience for foolishness in any way, shape, or form. But he was also a good listener and oftentimes gave excellent advice.

What would he say when Rory told him that he had fallen in love with a servant? Would he be disappointed with him, like his mother so obviously was? She barely looked him in the eye these past weeks.

She was so intent on him marrying Georgiana that she wasn't about to let a servant interrupt her plans. And Lady Kinkade was a more realistic choice as a bride, but he wanted Shannon to be his wife, and he was tired of hiding their love.

He knew what the *ton* would say. Knew that he would fall from grace, and thereby put his family in an unfavorable light, but he had faith that his brothers would ultimately back him. After all, they had married women they had both fallen in love with.

Why should it be any different for him?

Perhaps his father would surprise him and let Rory follow his own heart.

Rory made sure to keep pace with the others, even though Georgiana seemed more than determined to fall behind.

When Claymoore Hall came into view, he breathed a sigh of relief. Already he could not wait to see Shannon and tell her his plans.

A few of the footmen came out to assist them, but Zachary was not among them.

"I would like to freshen up before dinner. I'll see you shortly," he said to Georgiana.

"Very well," Georgiana said, looking pleased and anxious.

He left her at the foyer and climbed the steps to his chamber, hoping that Shannon would be there waiting for him, but she wasn't.

His valet had laid out a black suit for tonight's festivities. He removed his cravat and rested it over the back of a chair, then followed with his shirt, his gaze shifting to the rug where he'd made love to Shannon last night.

He was tired of stolen moments. He wanted the luxury of going to bed with her each night and waking up with her in his arms each morning. He didn't want the other servants whispering behind her back, or Lady Kinkade watching her with despite. He wanted to call her wife.

Though Shannon loved the outdoors, being outside in the dark with no light to guide her way, and nothing but a cloak to cover her, was nothing short of miserable.

Even worse, she had heard earlier that a storm was coming.

"We need to find cover soon," she said, struggling under the weight of the reticule she had brought along. The bag contained a change of clothing, apples she had picked in an orchard they had crossed, a loaf of bread, a hairbrush, and soap. Zachary's pack was far heavier, and yet he didn't seem to be struggling as much.

He could travel farther and faster without her, and there had been a few times she had nearly told him to go on without her. At least a hundred times she had thought about running straight back to Claymoore Hall and to Rory. A life on the run, taking odd jobs where they could find them, compared to a life as a mistress. True, she would always have to watch out for her cousin, but what if she told Rory the truth? Maybe he could take care of matters once and for all and protect them.

A crack of thunder came, and lightning filled the sky, showing an old, neglected shack in the distance. If anything, it would be a dry place to lay their heads for the night.

The shack had been long ago abandoned, with holes in the floors and walls, and it was obvious animals had used the place for shelter. Shannon hoped none was there now.

At least it would give shelter from the rain. Using her reticule as a pillow, she lay down beside her brother.

Tears tightened her throat as she tried not to think about what Rory was doing at the moment. Did he even realize that she had left yet, or was he too occupied with Georgiana to notice?

"Zachary?"

"Yeah?"

"What if we told someone about Clint? I mean . . . what if we told Rory or Lady Graston the truth? We could have him arrested, and perhaps then we could get our lives back."

"We just keep going as we have been. Everything will be fine. You'll see. You just need to have faith."

"But I know that Rory would have helped us. Lady or Lord Graston as well. We should have at least tried." She swallowed past the lump in her throat. "We are not so far away that we can't return."

"And run the risk of coming across Clinton. I think not."

She pressed her lips together and pulled the coat tighter about her.

"You'll like Scotland, Shannon," he said, his voice softer than moments before. "We'll be happy there."

"Will we really?"

His brows furrowed. "Of course."

"I'm not so sure anymore."

"Sister, you must put these silly thoughts aside. Lord Ambrose is going to marry Lady Kinkade. You would be nothing but his plaything until he tired of you. If we had stayed, Clinton would have found us and killed us. Now we at least have a chance at a life, such as it is."

Yes, but how long until he would find them again? How long before they would have to start running?

Lightning lit the sky and she shivered, wishing more than anything she were at Claymoore Hall in the safety of Rory's arms.

Shannon was gone.

Her reticule was missing. She'd left no note, neither had Zachary. The two had left while the family had been out at the abbey, and no one had noticed until nightfall when Georgiana had awoken from her nap. As she'd been readying for dinner she had noticed that her emerald necklace and earrings were missing.

All the servants had been assembled and questioned, and Shannon and Zachary were gone.

Rory didn't believe that Shannon or Zachary had stolen Lady

Kinkade's jewels, but why then would she have left while they'd all been gone?

It did not bode well.

A thorough search of the grounds proved that Shannon and Zachary had left . . . and on foot, since none of the horses was missing.

Which meant they wouldn't have gotten too far. But which direction did they go?

"The two could not have gone far," Betsy said, taking a sip of chocolate. "I honestly did not take them as thieves. They seemed so genuinely happy with Lillith and Victor."

Lillith stood by the window, staring out. "They are not thieves, Lady Rochester. Shannon and Zachary would never steal."

"Their absence and the disappearance of my jewels can hardly be coincidence," Georgiana said, an odd gleam in her eye.

"Perhaps you misplaced them, Lady Kinkade," Lillith said, turning toward the other woman.

Georgiana lifted her chin. "I did not misplace my jewels, Lady Graston."

"Shannon would not have—"

"How do you know what she would or would not have done?" Georgiana's face was red with fury. "Did you know her that well?"

"Come, all this bickering is not going to help find them," Victor said, sliding a hand around his wife's shoulders.

"We shall find them, bring them back, and then we will have all the time to question them."

"I would let the authorities question them," Georgiana said.

Rory noticed Lillith bit her lip and looked away.

"I am not just going to sit here," Rory said, heading to his chamber to change, a thousand different emotions rushing through him, most of all, anger and guilt. He should have insisted Shannon talk to him. She had said she would tell him about her past when they had time to do so. He just never had made time. And yet he'd had time to make love to her.

"Why do you not just let the others go?"

Rory glanced up at the doorway, surprised to find Georgiana had followed him to his chamber, and now she stood at the door with arms crossed over her chest. He had seen the look of triumph in her eye when the first alarm had been raised before supper. Now, hours later, she seemed incredibly confident, and he didn't like it.

"Why are you chasing her?" she demanded.

"Because I have to."

She took a step farther into the room. "You are being foolish, Rory. She is a servant."

"I don't care."

"You are in lust."

"I am in love!"

Her eyes widened. "Love? No, you confuse lust with love."

"Do you not think I know the difference?"

She shook her head. "You are a fool. Everyone will laugh at you."

"Let them laugh. I honestly do not care."

"Love her or not, I will see her hang," she said through clenched teeth, and with a frustrated cry, rushed out of the room.

Rory finished changing and, hearing a carriage arrive, rushed down the stairs, praying it was Shannon.

Jeffries, Lord and Lady Rochester's valet, opened the front door, and Marilyn lowered the hood of her cloak and he swallowed his disappointment. To his surprise, Anna followed behind her.

"Is Shannon here?" Marilyn asked, her eyes wide with concern.

His heart jolted. "No, she and her brother have left."

"Oh dear," Anna said with a heavy sigh.

"What do you know?" he asked, taking the steps that separated them.

Victor and Sinjin quickly joined them on the landing.

Anna pulled a newspaper clipping from her pocket. "Rory, you asked me to find out information about Clinton O'Connor, and I did. I had a discussion with him that made me very uneasy, and I went to the library to see what I could find. I found this."

She handed him a newspaper clipping, and Rory read,

Prominent Dublin businessman and family perish in deadly fire. Earl O'Connor, Ennis O'Connor, and their children, daughter Shannon, and son Zachary, all died in the blaze that destroyed the family's Dublin mansion. Four servants perished in the blaze as well. Clinton O'Connor, nephew, was not at home at the time of the fire.

Rory felt his throat tighten. Shannon had dreamt about the fire. The fear he'd seen on her face when she'd walked into the dining room and saw her cousin. It all made sense now.

"Oh my God," Victor said, brushing a hand through his hair, looking at Rory with disbelief. "So you believe the cousin is responsible for setting the fire, and now he is after Shannon and Zachary?"

"Exactly, I went to his hotel in London and he had checked out . . . the very day you left for Claymoore Hall."

"Where would they have gone?" Rory said, more determined than ever to find her.

"I do not know," Anna replied. "I am sorry, Rory. I wish I'd found out sooner. I know how very much you care for Shannon."

"How scared they must be," Lillith said, looking on the verge of tears. "I knew something was wrong, but I did not push. I should have. I should have insisted she tell me the truth."

Rory shook his head. "I should have known."

"There is not time to blame ourselves," Victor said matter-of-factly. "We must help them now."

"I imagine on foot they could not have gotten too far. We can each take a different road and see if we have any luck."

Katelyn walked in, with Johnny in tow.

"Marilyn," Katelyn said, hugging her sister to her.

"Johnny, tell them what you told me," Katelyn said to the young man.

Rory straightened, almost fearful of what was about to come out of the lad's mouth. He knew he had feelings for Shannon.

"Well, when we were still in Twickenham, I overheard Shannon and Zachary talking in the stable," he said, looking nervous. "Zachary said something about going to Paris, but Shannon didn't want to leave London. Then Scotland was mentioned, and they both agreed that they would be happier there. That it would be more like Ireland."

"Can you remember anything else?"

Johnny chewed his lower lip. "Yes, this afternoon, why ye were gone, I saw them rush for the tree line, toward the lake. They were on foot. I yelled after them, but they didn't look back . . . and I know they heard me."

"Thank you for your help," Rory said, hope building within his chest.

The other man nodded. He started for the door, then turned back at Rory. "I want to help look for them."

Rory nodded. "We can use all the help we can get."

"I'll get my things," Johnny said, rushing out the door.

"Father has maps in his study," Victor said.

"Thank you, Anna," Rory said, giving her a hug. "You are a good friend."

"As are you," she said, kissing his cheek. "You'll find her. I feel it in my bones."

"I hope you are right."

"Come, you both must be exhausted," Lillith said, taking Anna and Marilyn by the hand. "Jeffries, could you please bring us some tea in the red parlor?"

"Of course, my lady. Straightaway."

"I'll be in the study with Vic and Rory," Sinjin said, and Katelyn nodded as she followed the women.

27

Shannon heard the slow creak of the door, and her breath caught in her throat. She glanced at Zachary, who was snoring, his back to her. Dawn was fast approaching, the blackness giving way to gray.

The entire night she had tossed and turned, unable to quiet her thoughts long enough to sleep longer than minutes at a stretch, every little sound waking her.

She closed her eyes and tried to get comfortable, drawing her cloak tight about her shoulders. Try as she might, she could not keep her mind from drifting back to Rory. What she wouldn't give to be in his arms now. Though she wanted to be his wife, the offer of mistress didn't seem like a terrible alternative at the moment. In fact, it was all she could do not to run back into his arms. They had not traveled so very far, after all. Maybe five hours on—

A board creaked, and before she could move, a hand slid about her neck, fingers tightening, while another hand firmly clamped over her mouth. Heart pumping like mad, her eyes widened and she stared into the familiar eyes of her cousin.

"Did you honestly think you could escape without me finding you?" he said, his eyes glittering in the darkness.

His hand was smashed over her nose, making her fight for breath. He covered her with his lower body, hooking his leg tight about her, making movement impossible.

She tried to struggle, but her efforts only made him angrier, the fingers at her neck tightening. She was losing consciousness quickly. He must have realized as much because he released his hold, but only slightly. "I will remove my hand from your mouth, but you must not utter a word or I shall kill you. Understand?"

Shannon nodded, and when he lifted his hand, she remained silent, fearful of him following through on his threat.

Her brother continued to snore. *Zachary, wake up!*

"What do you want from us?" she asked.

"I want to bring your brother to justice . . . for the death of your parents." His voice was very matter-of-fact.

Her pulse skittered. "What do you mean?"

Rearing back, he looked down at her, his brows furrowed. "Zachary set the fire, Shannon," he whispered, glancing toward her brother's inert form. "Did you not wonder why he was so desperate to flee Ireland?"

"We saw you the night of the fire, Clinton. Standing in the shadows doing nothing while you watched the mansion burn while we were in it."

"Zachary would say that, wouldn't he?"

She stared at him, her mind racing. "Why would he kill his own parents? That makes no sense."

"He was jealous because your father was molding me to take over the family business."

Zachary had never said as much to her, and she had a hard time believing that their father would have ever overlooked his own son for his nephew. If anything, Zachary had always felt a certain pressure that his life was already mapped out for him.

"Why would he save me from the fire, then?"

"He has no anger toward you, Shannon. You're not a threat to him. Don't you see . . . you were not involved in the business in any way."

"Then he would have saved Mother, too, if that were the case."

"Get your hands off of her, you murderer," Zachary said through clenched teeth. "How dare you try to fill her head with such wicked thoughts? You are a fiend."

Clinton's eyes narrowed. "Who are you calling murderer?"

"I did not set that fire, and well you know it."

"We all know the truth of it. You are guilty, Zachary, and soon you will pay for their murders."

Clinton held Shannon tight to him, a knife at her neck. She felt the tip break the skin.

"Release her now, Clinton. She serves you no purpose."

"I will not release her."

A nerve in Zachary's neck jumped. "I will kill you if you don't release her now." His voice was deadly calm, but she could clearly see the fury in his eyes.

"See," Clinton whispered against her ear. "He is full of murderous rage. Do you not wonder why he wanted to leave the safety and security of Claymoore Hall? He knew in time you'd discover the truth."

"Do not listen to him, Shannon."

She knew her brother better than anyone, and didn't for a moment believe Clinton, but she wondered if he had told anyone else that Zachary was responsible for their parents' deaths? Dear God, what if he had convinced others that Zachary was responsible and her brother was ultimately charged for their murders?

"What do you want from us?" Zachary asked, his gaze skipping between her and Clinton. She could tell he was scared, though he was doing his best not to show it.

"What do you think, Zachary? We will return to Ireland where you will stand trial for your parents' murders."

"You are pathetic," Zachary said, fury in his eyes. "If I was the killer, why then would you not just let me go? You are the sole heir."

Shannon felt him stiffen. "Not everyone is convinced you are dead. However, I can take care of that."

The darkness of the shelter gave way to gray as the sun came up. Even if one of them were able to get away and make their way back to Claymoore Hall, then they could bring help back to the other.

Shannon looked at her brother and motioned with her eyes for him to go.

He frowned.

"Go," she mouthed the word, and Clinton promptly pulled back on her, choking her as he did.

"If you even think of fleeing, Zachary, I will slit her throat. Don't think that I won't."

Zachary lifted his chin, his throat convulsing as he swallowed hard. "Let her go. It is me that you want."

"Actually, I need you *both* dead."

Fear rushed up her spine. He was insane, and he would finish what he had started. She had no doubt of that.

"She will not say anything to anyone, will you, Shannon?" Zachary said in a surprisingly calm voice. "She can go about her life and be fine. No one need know the truth."

Clinton's false laughter filled the shed. "I'll know that you are alive, though . . . and I don't need that constant threat."

"And here I thought you said Zachary set the blaze."

"Bitch," he said, squeezing her neck so tight she started choking.

"Leave her alone!" Zachary said, knocking the blade from his hand.

He took Clinton so much by surprise that the other man faltered and gave her enough time to slip from his grasp.

"Go!" Zachary said, motioning toward the door.

"I won't leave you."

"I said go!" he yelled, his eyes intense.

"I'll fuckin' kill you," Clinton said, swiping at the blood on his lip, while he clutched the knife with the other.

Zachary had no weapon.

Shannon rushed for the door and Clinton raced after her. She stumbled and fell, nearly knocking her head on a rack near the door.

She got to her feet and made it the door, but hesitated. She couldn't possibly leave Zachary with this madman. Their cousin was physically stronger than Zachary and could easily overpower him.

Zachary threw a punch, which connected with Clinton's jaw.

Clinton hit him in return, and Zachary stumbled back a few feet, putting a hand to his cut lip. He looked at her. "Run!"

Shannon ran like the devil was on her heels.

She kept to the trees and heavy brush, constantly looking over her shoulder and listening for her cousin.

Her heart was a roar in her ears as she tried to remember the way they had come, while trying not to think what was happening back at the shack.

Poor Zachary.

"Shannon!" The cry came from a long way away, but she

heard it. She stopped in her tracks and closed her eyes, concentrating on the direction it had come from as her name was shouted yet again.

Her heart leapt to her throat.

It was Clinton, not Zachary. A chill rushed up her spine. She was close to the road. She could even hear an approaching carriage. Breaking into a run, she raced for the road and the carriage.

She heard a curse behind her, could hear the sound of him running in her direction. Glancing back, she could see where her footsteps had made a path in the dew-covered grass.

Worse still, her skirts hampered her progress, but she lifted them to her thighs and ran for all she was worth. "Help!" she yelled, and swore she heard the carriage start to slow down.

"Help me!" she screamed louder, seeing the road now and the approaching carriage. The driver was looking into the trees frantically, and in the carriage, a man and woman stared out the windows. Behind them was another carriage.

She would be safe . . . *if* she could make it to the road before Clinton caught her.

Something whizzed by her head and she ducked just in time. A knife lay lodged in a nearby tree. The same knife Clinton had held at her throat now rested deep in the bark.

He couldn't be far away.

"Help!" she said, breaking through the trees and onto the road. The coachman's eyes widened in surprise and he brought the horses to a halt. The man inside the carriage opened the door and rushed toward her, while the driver scurried down, a rifle in hand, his gaze scouring the woods.

"Who is after you?" the man urged. He was at least fifty years old and dressed in the clothing of a gentleman.

"His name is Clinton O'Connor. My cousin. He killed my parents and he has my brother."

"Good God," the woman in the carriage said. "How utterly terrifying."

As the other carriage pulled up alongside, three men poured out. "What is it, my lord?"

"This woman is being pursued by a man."

"He is through there," she said, pointing in the direction she had just come. "Be careful. He threw a knife at me, and I have no idea if he has other weapons on his person."

A man rushed over to the tree and pulled the knife out. "Fetch my pistol," he said, and the driver did exactly that.

"I have to go to my brother," Shannon said, relieved that she had found help but still terrified for her brother. "My cousin has him hostage in a shack not far from here."

"Can we get there by carriage?" the woman asked.

"I do not know. If we go north and then break west, perhaps."

The gentleman shook his head. "I will not put you in harm's way, my dear. Plus, this poor girl has been through enough. You will stay here, and Marcus will stand guard. I shall send Travis ahead. He is the fastest rider, and we will follow on horseback, scouring the woods in case he's hiding amongst the trees."

The woman motioned Shannon into the carriage. "My dear girl, what you must have gone through, I can only imagine." She gave a shudder.

"Marcus, pull the carriage off the road. Unhook two of the team."

"Be careful, my love," the woman said to her husband.

He nodded and looked at Shannon. "We shall get this scoundrel. Rest assured."

Rory saw the carriages ahead of him in the roadway and had a feeling that they had finally found Shannon. A mixture of fear and excitement rushed through his veins, and he prayed that she was alive.

"My lord," Johnny said, nodding toward a man who walked toward them, gun pointed square at their chests.

The young footman had insisted on traveling with him, and Rory had been grateful for his help, especially given he was the one who had last seen Zachary and Shannon. He had been an excellent tracker too. He said he'd spent long days in the highlands with his father, securing meat for his master's table.

They had tracked Shannon and Zachary's footsteps for a few miles, but once they came to the river, they'd lost them and had traveled to the main road.

"We are looking for a woman," Rory said, approaching the man, who did not lower the gun.

"Who are you?" the beefy man asked.

"Lord Ambrose, and this is Johnny. We are searching for a young woman named Shannon O'Connor."

"What does this girl look like?"

"Pale blond hair, light blue eyes, black cloak."

"Are you the cousin?"

"No, I am her fiancé," Rory replied, and Johnny's eyes widened.

"Where is the woman?"

The man shifted the gun so it was no longer pointed toward them. "There," he said, motioning to the first carriage in line, where a driver stood on the perch, rifle in hand, scanning the area.

"Shannon," Rory shouted, and he heard her cry out.

"Rory!" She came rushing from the carriage, her hair a tangled mess, tears staining her cheeks.

Relief washed over him as he met her halfway and held her tight in his arms. "Shannon, you are all right. Thank God."

"Clinton has found us, Rory," she said, fear shining in her

eyes. "My cousin who killed my parents and now he wants us dead. I think he's hurt Zachary."

Rory's heart dropped to his feet. "Where is Zachary?"

"I left him back at an old shack through the trees." She pointed to the northwest. "If you head past the clearing, you should see it."

"My husband and some of our men have gone in pursuit," the lady said from the carriage. "They will find him."

"Will you be all right here?" Rory asked, kissing Shannon's forehead. He really didn't want to leave her, but he needed to find Zachary and fast.

"Yes."

"We have Marcus," the lady said. "He has a sharp eye, and I will not let any harm come to her. You have my word on it."

Making sure Shannon was settled back in the carriage, Rory mounted his horse and waited for Johnny to do the same.

"Be careful, Rory. He's crazy . . . and desperate."

28

Rory found Clinton within a quarter of an hour. He lay sprawled facedown on the ground, his hands tied behind his back.

"Where is Zachary?" Rory asked him, only to receive a sneer for his trouble.

Rory dismounted, grabbed him by the back of the neck, and lifted him off the ground. "I asked you where Zachary is."

Clinton spit on him.

Rage made him want to snap the man in two. Wiping the spit off his face with his free hand, Rory released him, and Clinton laughed under his breath.

The gentleman approached him and introduced himself as Samuel Clemens. "He has blood on his right hand," Samuel said, and Rory could read the concern in his eyes.

A shiver rushed along his spine. "Where is the shack, Clinton? In which direction?"

Clinton said nothing.

"Do you know the area?" Rory asked the gentleman.

"The only shack I can think of is an old hunting cabin near the lake."

"Let's go."

Rory went down on his haunches beside Clinton. "If you have touched one hair on his head, I will kill you."

"You should be thanking me. Zachary is the one who killed his parents."

The men around Rory took a collective breath.

"No," Rory said. "You are a liar. Do not try to pass off your cruel deeds on another."

"Zachary set fire to the family home so that he would inherit everything." Clinton didn't so much as blink. "He was jealous of me. Mad that his father had given me so much power."

The accusation took Rory aback. "Why did Shannon flee, then?"

"Shannon didn't know her brother was responsible for the murders. I told her to run because I was afraid he would kill her as well since she knows the truth. He wants us both dead so that no one will know his secret."

Johnny shook his head and walked toward his horse. "I will not stay a minute longer and listen to lies. I'm going to find the shack."

Rory nodded.

"So Zachary ran in fear?" Samuel said, giving Rory a look that said to play along.

"Yes, he was desperate. He took his sister as leverage, but in time he had her believing it was me who was responsible."

"Tell us where he is. We'll go after him," Samuel said, sounding cautious.

Clinton's gaze shifted between Samuel and Rory, and his eyes narrowed seconds before he cursed under his breath.

Shannon couldn't stand to wait in the carriage another minute. She had to see her brother or go mad. "Please, let me take a horse and go to him."

Mrs. Clemens shook her head. "I cannot be responsible if something happens to you, my dear."

"The men are already far ahead of me. Surely they have found my cousin by now. I don't care about him. I care about my brother. I cannot sit here and do nothing."

The older woman bit her lip in indecision. "And I do not blame you. I would want to know my brother's whereabouts as well."

Shannon could tell Gladys was wavering. "I will tell Mr. Clemens that I ran before you could stop me."

"You had better, because my husband will be furious with me." Mrs. Clemens stepped out of the carriage with Shannon and looked at Marcus. "Go with her, Marcus. I shall take full responsibility."

Marcus broached no argument and did as she said. He unbridled one of the horses and Shannon climbed behind the beefy servant.

"Thank you, Mrs. Clemens. I shall never forget your kindness."

"Just come back safe, my dear," Mrs. Clemens said, looking ready to change her mind.

Having ridden all her life, Shannon wanted desperately to take the reins and fly across the clearing, but all she could do was hold on to Marcus as he eased the mare into a gallop.

She could see nothing but the passing landscape, but soon he was slowing. It was then she recognized the pathway she had cut through the trees.

The one that led to the shack.

Her stomach lurched.

She very nearly let out a scream when she saw her cousin and then released a breath when she realized he was tied to a tree, and a man was standing guard with a rifle leveled at chest level.

Seeing Shannon, Clinton's eyes widened.

Why was it so quiet? Especially given the fact there were so many of them in the shack.

"Zachary!" she yelled, pulling on the reins and jumping off the horse.

She was met at the door by Johnny. "No, Shannon. Ye don't want to see him."

Her heart lurched in her chest. "What do you mean?"

"It's bad," he said, his voice breaking.

She tried to look over his shoulder, but he blocked her.

"I want to see my brother."

"He's dead, Shannon," Clinton said from where he stood nearby, chewing on a nail, his lips curved in a malicious smile.

Zachary was dead? She wavered on her feet, and Rory appeared, taking her in his arms.

A guttural moan caught in her throat and she couldn't breathe.

"Shh, it's okay," he said, holding her tight. "He's not dead, but he's lost a lot of blood, Shannon." His blue eyes were full of concern. "I don't know if he's going to make it."

"I want to see him," she said, her hands gripping the collar of his shirt. "Please, Rory. Let me see my brother."

His gaze searched hers, and she could see the indecision in his face, the fear that she would not take whatever she was about to see well.

He nodded and released her. She rushed past Johnny and the others, who made a pathway.

Zachary lay with Rory's jacket beneath his head. The lower half of his white linen shirt was soaked with blood, which was frightening, since from what Shannon could tell, the point of entry had been near his groin. His black pants were soaked with blood, too, as was the floor beneath him.

"We can move him to my estate. I am renting a home a few

miles from here," Mr. Clemens said. "I will send for the surgeon."

"Zachary," Shannon said, brushing his hair off his forehead.

He was so pale, his lips already had a purplish hue to them. His eyes fluttered open. Seeing her, his lips curved slightly. "You're alive."

"Yes, I'm alive, and so are you. We'll be all right, Zach. Once you have recovered, we can return to Ireland and start over."

"I didn't kill them," he said the words so softly she barely heard them.

"I know, Zach. I know. Clinton is a liar and a murderer, and he shall pay for what he has done." Tears blinded her and she blinked them away.

"Shannon, time is of the essence," Rory said from behind her. "Zachary, we are moving you to Mr. Clemens's home. He lives nearby and it will not take long."

"Do not bother. I am dying."

"No," Shannon said adamantly. "You will live."

His eyes closed, as though he did not have the strength to keep them open, and Shannon looked at Rory with all the helplessness she felt.

"Zachary, they will be extremely careful, but you must be strong," she said.

If he heard her, he gave no indication, slipping into unconsciousness.

The men slid him onto a blanket and lifted him.

"Please hurry," Shannon said, fearful of the time it would take to return to the carriages and then onto the manor.

She followed the group out of the shack and stopped short seeing her cousin.

Seeing her, his lips curled into a triumphant smile. He looked maniacal, his eyes wild. "Ah, poor little Shannon. Soon ye will be all alone. No parents, no brother, nothing."

"How could you be so cruel?" she asked, not expecting an answer.

He merely shrugged.

"What do we do with him?" Marcus asked Rory, and Rory looked to Shannon.

"If I had my way, we'd hang him from the nearest tree," Johnny said under his breath, blinking back tears as he watched his friend being carried out of the shack. "Or I'm happy to put a bullet in his black heart."

"No," Shannon said. "Death is too easy." Shannon thought back over the years of all that her parents had done for him. Of the times that she, Clinton, and Zachary had played in the fields near their Dublin mansion, how the entire family had embraced him so readily.

"You will be an orphan," Clinton said again, laughing under his breath.

"That is where you are wrong." Rory slid a hand around Shannon's shoulders. "Shannon is part of my family now, as is Zachary, and you will rot in prison for what you have done."

29

Marilyn looked out the window at the fading light, then turned to her aunt, who had been silent for the past hour since retiring to her chamber.

Despite Lord Rochester's arrival at Claymoore Hall, the overall uneasiness of the mansion's occupants had a sobering affect on everyone.

Lillith had greeted her father-in-law with warmth but had been unable to keep from pacing the length of the parlor. Lady Rochester had suggested a bath with lavender, but she had declined.

"They should have heard something by now. Why have we not heard anything?" Katelyn said, her hand splaying over her slightly swollen belly.

"Dear, please sit down," Lillith said, motioning for her to take the seat beside her. "You are not doing the child any good by fretting."

Anna took a long swig of brandy. "If only I had come earlier."

"Do not be silly. Had you not come at all, then we would

not know the danger that Shannon and Zachary were in," Lillith said earnestly.

"She is right." Katelyn patted Anna on the shoulder. "You are a good friend, and I am glad you are here."

"Thank you," Anna replied.

Marilyn smiled at her sister, grateful for her compassion. On the long ride here, she had come to accept that Anna would never be anything more than her friend, and she was at peace with that. It seemed they both were, as Anna had talked incessantly about her American beau and how she was ready to leave England behind. She had even invited Marilyn to come visit, but she knew that the visit would never happen. Her place was with Stanley. Sweet Stanley who had constantly stood up for her regardless of his family's lack of acceptance.

How she missed him.

Katelyn joined her at the window and looked out. She squinted and leaned closer, her head making contact with the glass.

"Do you see something?" Lillith asked, rushing toward her.

"Yes, it's two riders," she said, excitement in her voice.

Anna joined them at the window, standing on her toes so that she could see over Marilyn's shoulder.

"It is Sinjin!" Katelyn was already rushing toward the door.

All of them flew downstairs and were met in the landing by Lady and Lord Rochester, who looked as anxious as they were. Sinjin walked in, his gaze going to Katelyn, who rushed into his awaiting arms.

"Well, what news?" Lord Rochester asked.

"Nothing." He kissed his wife on the forehead and looked around at the somber group. "Do not tell me I am the first one to return?"

Betsy nodded. "I fear you are, my dear boy."

Lord Rochester squeezed her shoulders. "Do not fret. Victor and Rory shall return with Shannon and Zachary, and when they do, we will be waiting for them."

Sinjin embraced his father, and Anna ran a hand down her face. "I am tired. I shall be in my chamber if you hear anything. Please let me know when you do."

Marilyn nodded and watched her go, worried about her friend's well-being. She had been extremely quiet since arriving on her doorstep with the news about Shannon and Zachary.

Shannon had fallen asleep in the chair beside her brother. The surgeon had done all that he could, and now Zachary's life was in God's hands. He had lost an enormous amount of blood, the surgeon had said, and he did not know if he would live through the night.

Even a priest had been called to deliver Last Rites.

Rory put an arm around her shoulder and she leaned into him, resting her cheek against his chest. "I cannot lose him, Rory. I cannot."

"You should go to bed." His hand slid up and down her arm in an effort to comfort her. He'd been a rock since coming on the scene yesterday, and she was so incredibly grateful for his presence. "You need to rest, my love. Mrs. Clemens has set up a chamber for you."

"No, I cannot leave him. I will not leave him."

"You will not be of service to him if you are exhausted."

"Have you sent word to your family to let them know where you are?" she asked, knowing Lord Graston and his family would be beside themselves with worry.

"Johnny has returned to Claymoore Hall to tell the others that you have been found."

She nodded, glad to know the family had received word. "What happened to Clinton?"

"The men took him into custody. From what I understand, he will be transported back to Ireland soon."

The fury she felt toward her cousin ran deep, and whatever happened to him, he had sealed his own fate. "I will never understand how he could have done something so horrific, and to the only family he has ever known."

"Greed does strange things to a person. I'm sorry, Shannon. If I could take your pain away, I would."

"I know." She slid her arms around his waist, taking the comfort he offered, savoring the feelings of being in his strong arms. "I'm sorry I was not honest with you from the very beginning. I wanted to tell you the truth, but I promised Zachary that I wouldn't."

He kissed the top of her head. "I understand. You did what you had to in order to survive." Had she just been honest, the outcome could have been so very different.

"I would do the same for my brothers."

"I don't want to lose him, Rory," she said, once again speaking her fears aloud.

He held her close, his hand moving up and down her back. "There's nothing we can do but wait now."

Sliding his free hand in hers, he brought it to his lips. "And now I must insist you get some rest. If only for a little while. I shall alert you the second he opens his eyes."

She took a seat in the chair beside the bed. "I'll rest my eyes for just a second," she said.

She was asleep within minutes.

Rory woke to the sun shining straight into his eyes. He lay on the settee in the Clemens's guest room. Shannon was on her knees beside the bed, her hands wrapped around her brother's hand.

His heart gave a lurch. Dear Lord, had the boy died during the night?

Shannon turned and looked at him, a wide smile on her face. "He woke just minutes ago. His breathing is so shallow."

Zachary was extremely pale and looked barely able to keep his eyes open.

"What of the surgeon?"

"On his way," she said, hope shining in her beautiful eyes.

Zachary blinked a few times and glanced at Rory. "Thank ye." His voice was hoarse, but Rory could not help but smile because he had clearly heard the boy's true accent come through.

"Clinton?" he asked, struggling to swallow.

"Will soon be on his way to Dublin to account for all he has done," Shannon said, not hiding her anger. "We will have our lives back now, Zach. We will return to Dublin and start over."

"Yes," Zachary said, closing his eyes once more, but the slight smile remained on his lips. "We shall rebuild the manor."

A knock sounded at the door, and Shannon stood.

Mrs. Clemens appeared, an anxious expression on her face, and the surgeon was fast on her heels. The baldheaded man rushed into the room and looked stunned to see Zachary awake and alert.

"How are you, young man?"

"Alive," Zachary replied, the word barely more than a whisper.

"Come, let us allow the physician to do his job," Mrs. Clemens said, motioning for Shannon and Rory to follow her from the room.

They stood outside the chamber with Mrs. Clemens and Rory, who was thankful for the older woman's wonderful gift of conversation. The time flew and soon the physician stepped from the room.

"He needs a lot of rest," he said, and Shannon could tell by his expression that her brother was not yet out of the woods.

"Of course, and he shall have it," Mrs. Clemens said matter-of-factly. "No one will be allowed to disturb him."

"He is not able to move the limb at all, and I honestly do not know if he will ever regain use of it again." The physician glanced at Shannon. "Only time will tell."

Rory felt sick to his stomach. If he could not use his leg, then he could not walk, and the boy had not reached his seventeenth birthday.

Shannon had gone pale, and he squeezed her hand in reassurance.

"We must be vigilant when it comes to fever," the doctor said. "The last thing he can afford is infection."

"We shall keep a close eye on him." Rory extended his hand to the other man, who took it.

The physician nodded. "He has asked to have a moment alone with you, Lord Ambrose, but I urge you to keep it brief. He needs to rest."

"Of course. I'll be right back," Rory said, giving Shannon's hand a squeeze before walking into the room. The physician had pulled the heavy drapes and a candle gave off a small amount of light.

Zachary sat up the slightest bit, a pillow beneath his back. He looked incredibly uncomfortable, and Rory silently commiserated with the young man. Having been in a similar situation not so long ago, he knew the pain involved. However, Zachary's wound was far graver than Rory's, and it would take a long time for him to heal.

"You wished to speak with me?" Rory said, sitting down in the chair.

Zachary opened his eyes. "Aye. What are your intentions with my sister?"

Rory smiled. That was not the question he had expected. "I wish to marry her . . . with your permission."

"She said ye asked her to be your mistress."

"I made a mistake," Rory said sheepishly. "For that I am sorry."

"She's in love with you, ye know."

His stomach clenched, and the words filled him with joy. "Did she tell you as much?"

"Aye, she did."

"I love her, too, and I'll make her extremely happy."

"Ye had better." He tried to get comfortable but gave up with a sigh. When Rory tried to help, he shook his head. "She is the only family I have left."

"No, she's not."

His brows furrowed. "I will marry your sister, Zach, and soon my family will be your family."

The sides of his mouth curved. "I would like that."

"I want you to know that you'll never have to worry about having a home. You can stay with us for as long as you want."

"Thank ye, Rory, but Ireland is where I belong."

He understood the boy's need to return to his roots and begin again. He just hoped that Shannon would understand and be at peace with her brother's decision.

"I hope we can move you to Claymoore Hall soon. You need time to convalesce."

His gaze shifted toward his legs. "The physician said I could have trouble walking."

Rory saw the fear in the boy's eyes. "I understand there might be damage to the nerves."

"What will I do if I can't walk or ride my horse?"

"Nothing is for certain. The main thing you must focus on now is healing. Your sister is an excellent nurse, and I have a feeling she will not leave your side . . . even for an instant."

Zachary smiled softly, but Rory clearly saw the concern in the young man's eyes, and he made a pledge to himself that he would do everything in his power to help the boy regain that which he'd lost.

30

Marilyn watched the carriage drive out of sight, taking Lady Anna away from Claymoore Hall, back to London.

Stanley stood behind her, his hands on her shoulders. He had arrived at Claymoore Hall this morning, concerned by the news that had hit London a few days ago about Zachary.

He had come all this way for her, and seeing him, all windswept, his clothing splattered with dirt, concern for her and her family in his eyes, she had burst into tears, happy to have him with her.

When she had raced into his arms and held her tight, she knew that marrying him was the right decision. She had found her security in this man who would be her husband.

And everything would be all right. She felt it in her bones. Even more, when Anna had left without saying a word, Marilyn felt only a hint of sadness.

"You're trembling," Stanley whispered against her hair.

"Am I?" she asked, glancing back at him.

He was such a comfort to her, such a sweet soul, and she was so very thankful she had met him. Her loving baron. She reached up, took his hand in hers, and kissed his fingers.

"Thank you for coming," she said.

"I couldn't stay away."

"I'm glad you didn't."

He glanced past her to the carriage. "Do you love her, Marilyn? Do you love Lady Anna?"

Stanley was not stupid, and although she might have thought she'd kept her admiration for Anna private, he had obviously caught on to her affections. "I care for her as one does a friend."

His gaze returned to hers. "But nothing more?"

She shook her head. "Nothing more."

"When you had left London without a word, I thought perhaps you had left me for her."

"It is because of Anna that we discovered Clinton murdered Shannon and Zachary's parents."

"I know," he said, brushing his thumb over her lips, sending a shiver up her spine. "If you need time to decide about us—"

Her stomach clenched. "I've had more than enough time to ponder my future, and my future is you. I want to marry you. I want to be your wife, and I cannot wait to start our life together."

She saw the shock in his eyes, the love and adoration that had been there and grown with each meeting.

"I only wish that your parents shared your—"

"My parents have given their blessing, Marilyn," he said, his eyes dancing.

She watched him closely. "What?"

"My parents realized they were being brutish and bullheaded. They said they want my happiness . . . and they realize that my happiness requires that you are my wife."

She hugged him tight and pressed her cheek against his chest, flush against his fast beating heart.

His hand moved up and down her spine, and the hair on her arms stood on end. She lifted her face to his and he kissed her, his lips as soft as a butterfly's wings.

She deepened the kiss, and he moaned low in his throat and pulled her tightly against him. Feeling the heat of his cock against her, she cupped the high globes of his buttocks. "I want to make love to you."

He pulled away enough to look down at her, his brow furrowed.

"I want you, Stanley."

"But what of our wedding day?"

"It will still be special."

He swallowed hard. "What of the rest of the household?"

"They are far too busy with all the turmoil of late. They will not notice our absence. Plus, they think we are both resting. No one will come looking for us."

She started to unbutton his waistcoat and she knew he would not stop her.

"Lock the door."

He nearly stumbled over his feet in his haste. Walking toward her, he slid the jacket off and lay it over the back of a high-backed chair, then finished unbuttoning the waistcoat.

She turned her back to him and let him unbutton her dress, her heart racing nearly out of her chest.

The gown fell to her feet and she stepped out of it.

"Marilyn, are you absolutely certain?" he asked, his gaze devouring her, his hands hovering at the buttons on his trousers.

"I've never been so sure of anything," she said, smiling as she helped him with the buttons and pushed the pants past his hips. His cock stood at attention and her inner muscles tightened in anticipation of what was to come.

She sat on the settee and he followed her down, kissing her senseless. The feeling of his body covering hers was exquisite, and as he cupped his hips, she did likewise. He shifted slightly and looked down into her eyes. "I have a confession to make."

Her pulse skittered.

"I have never made love before."

She saw the vulnerability in his eyes, and it only endeared her to him even more, while guiding him into her slick entrance.

"We will be each other's first," she said as he slid inside.

From yet another window at Claymoore Hall, Lady Rochester watched the retreating carriage. She turned to Lillith, who played cards with Katelyn. "I never thought I would say this, but I have to admit that I'm rather happy to see that woman leave."

"I rather liked her," Lillith said, setting a card down on the table. She had come to enjoy her mother-in-law's company, even though she was extremely opinionated and didn't mind speaking her mind.

Katelyn frowned and picked another up on the stack. "I agree. Lady Anna has a good heart."

"I do not speak of Lady Anna, you two." Lady Rochester frowned at them both. "I meant Lady Kinkade. How dare she try to accuse our Shannon of stealing her jewels."

"Indeed," Lillith replied, eyes wide in surprise, still finding it hard to believe anyone would go to such lengths. "People do the oddest things when they are desperate."

Georgiana had been adamant that Shannon and Zachary had stolen her emerald necklace and earrings, and that was why they had left Claymoore Hall. Lillith had been fearful of the accusation, and being that they had fled with no reason had only added credence to the woman's claim. Thank goodness Greta, a housekeeper who had been sharing a room with Shannon, had stepped forward last night and said that she had seen Georgiana slip into her room and put something inside the dresser drawer beside Shannon's side of the bed. Greta had waited until the woman left to see what it was.

Greta said she had not come forward sooner for fear they would accuse her of stealing. Lillith could certainly understand the woman's concerns but was glad she had stepped forward to defend her employees.

When Greta had insisted that the woman in her room that night had been Georgiana, Lady Kinkade had flushed to the roots of her hair and denied any involvement, saying that Greta must be insane.

When Lord Rochester had suggested the magistrate be called in to deal with the matter, Georgiana had agreed for all of five minutes. Then she had graciously said not to bother, packed her bags, and left, conveniently with Lady Anna.

"I am certain Rory will be happy that she is no longer here," Katelyn said with a small smile, as she set a card down and took another from the deck.

"He never did like her, did he?" Lady Rochester said, falling into a nearby chair.

"I believe his heart was already taken by the time he met Lady Kinkade." Lillith glanced at her mother-in-law, who smiled.

"I knew he was in love with that girl the first time I saw them in the same room." A pleased smile teased the corners of her wrinkled mouth. "I have a feeling a marriage is on the horizon, my dears. Yes, indeed . . . I am a happy woman. Three daughters and a grandchild on the way."

Katelyn looked up at Lillith and cleared her throat.

Betsy glanced from one to the other. "What?"

Lillith lay the playing cards on the table. "I am pregnant, too, Mother Rochester."

Lady Rochester's brow pinched. "But I did not think you were able—" She clamped her lips shut.

"Nor did I, but I was wrong. I am going to have a child. I visited the physician before I left London. Victor and I wanted to wait until Lord Rochester arrived, but we have not felt that with everything going—"

Betsy was out of her chair and hugging Lillith the next second.

Lillith smiled over her shoulder at her niece, who had tears in her eyes.

"I am the happiest of mothers," she said, kissing Lillith's cheek. "Truly. I could not ask for anything more."

Nor could Lillith.

Lady Anna sat back against the velvet seat across from Lady Kinkade, who still looked agitated about being called out for trying to set up Shannon and Zachary.

On a whim, Anna had decided to leave Claymoore Hall too. She had realized since arriving at the manor that the curiosity that Marilyn might have felt about her had faded. That had become excruciatingly obvious when Stanley had arrived late last night.

Marilyn had been so excited, and the love she felt for the man so apparent to everyone, that Anna knew the right thing to do was to leave.

This doing the right thing was not so bad. Indeed, she rather liked how it made her feel.

"Do not look so grim, Lady Kinkade. There are other men besides Lord Ambrose in the world."

Georgiana sighed heavily. "But none so beautiful."

That was true. Of all the women she could have seen her friend end up with, she would have never anticipated Shannon O'Connor. How ironic that the girl had ended up not being a servant, after all, but a wealthy heiress.

Lucky, lucky girl.

"I hear you are to marry an American," Georgiana said, lifting a brow.

"I am not certain if I shall marry him or not." It seemed every few minutes she wavered.

"America is a long way away."

"Indeed." But the distance from England and her grandparents was not the only thing keeping her from saying yes to her American plantation owner.

Georgiana's eyes lit up. "You like someone?"

Was it that obvious? Since arriving at Claymoore Hall, she'd been unable to get Thomas out of her mind. At first she had thought perhaps it had to do with the fact she had first met him at the manor, but as the days went by, she realized what she felt for him was more than just friendship.

"Who is *he*?"

"A friend." Thomas was not a titled lord, but he was filthy rich, one criterion that her grandparents absolutely insisted on.

But would he marry her? He had gone to Claymoore Hall in order to find a wealthy bride, so why not her? Plus, they were so very good together. They liked all the same things, and no one could make her laugh like Thomas could.

"Come, I can keep a secret."

"Only if you tell me one of your own?"

The other woman pursed her lips and then sat forward, urging Anna to do the same. "Shake on it."

Anna shook her hand and a little shiver rushed up her spine.

Georgiana released her hand. "There is a man in Liverpool whom I love."

She knew Lady Kinkade had lived in Liverpool with her husband from the stories she had told while at Claymoore Hall.

"And?"

"You go."

Anna smiled slightly, liking the woman's spirit. "I have a friend, or rather a lover, who I think I would like to marry."

Georgiana licked her lips. "Go on."

"In fact, I think I love him." The admission shocked even her.

"I, too, have a lover."

Anna schooled her features. Lady Kinkade's reputation had been sterling. Not a blemish. "You must have been discreet."

"He lives in my household, so it is not so very difficult." Her gaze shifted to Anna's lips.

"A servant."

"No."

Anna saw the pulse beating erratically in the other woman's neck, the slight flush that rose to her cheeks. Kicking off her shoe, Anna slid her foot up the inside of her ankle.

Georgiana's breath caught in her throat.

"Who, then?" Anna asked, leaning forward, her hands pushing up the other woman's skirts and up her stockings that stopped at mid-thigh.

"My stepson," Georgiana said breathlessly, and Anna smiled inwardly.

"Oh, that is wonderfully scandalous, Lady Kinkade," Anna said, and Georgiana leaned forward. Their breath mingled. "And I mean that in the nicest possible way."

"You do not think me wicked?"

"It depends. How old is this stepson of yours—thirty?"

Lady Kinkade shook her head. "No."

"Twenty-five?" Anna said, lifting a brow when Georgina shook her head again.

"He is twenty. Six years younger than I."

"If men can do it, then why not women?"

Georgiana laughed under her breath. "Truthfully, Lady Anna, do you think me terribly wicked?"

Anna's lips touched hers, and she kissed her lightly. "No, I think you are a woman after my own heart," she whispered.

31

Shannon opened her eyes and found herself looking into brilliant blue eyes framed by lush, thick lashes.

Rory flashed a wolfish smile. "Good morning, wife."

She smiled at the declaration, at knowing this beautiful man, body and soul, was her husband, and that every single morning from this day on, she would go to bed in his arms and wake up in his arms. "Good morning, husband."

The small cabin was on the acreage at Claymoore Hall, an old hunting abode that had been used for generations by the Rayborne men. Lillith, Katelyn, and Marilyn had spent an entire afternoon decorating the one-room cabin in white lace and rose petals.

"I could stay here forever," Shannon said, brushing a lock of dark hair off his forehead.

"As could I."

The past week had been a time for celebration. Zachary had been moved from the Clemens's to Claymoore Hall, and the entire family had celebrated his return.

Lord Rochester even had a bit of color to his cheeks during

the ceremony, and Zachary had been well enough to attend the service that had taken place out on the verandah. Though he was still extremely weak, and could not move his leg very well, or walk, he talked of the future and his hope to one day see Ireland again.

Now, he was recovering in the west wing, being fawned over by the women of the household, particularly a pretty scullery maid whose mother worked as a housekeeper. On her day off she had wheeled Zachary about in a chair, and Shannon had watched them out in the gardens, drinking tea and playing cards. He seemed happier than he'd been in a very long time, and she had great faith that all would be right in their world.

"You are thinking of Zachary," Rory said, his hand moving down her ribs, making the hair on her arms stand on end.

"I am. He seems happy, and I'm so grateful to everyone for being so kind."

"He's going to be just fine. I know he will walk again."

"Aye, Johnny said he's making him crutches so that when he's strong enough, he can use them."

Johnny had been an enormous help and a wonderful friend to Rory. It seemed that he was the last to know about Shannon and Rory, and he had been disappointed, and even told her as much, but she knew he was also popular with the local girls and would find a mate worthy of his love and affection.

"The boy was in love with you."

Shannon shook her head. "No, he wasn't. Johnny is sweet, and I owe him a lot of gratitude for all that he has done for us."

Rory's brows lifted and she smiled, seeing jealousy in his eyes. "Do not fear. I love ye, my husband. No one ever could compare to you."

"Thank you for that," he said, kissing her gently. "I love you, too, and I love that brogue."

She knew he loved her. After all, he had fallen in love with her when she was just a servant. Lillith had told her that Rory had talked to his father about marrying her *before* he knew her true identity. The love she felt for him had grown even stronger with that knowledge.

"Thank you for everything. I owe you my life."

"Don't forget Mr. Clemens and his men," Rory said with a smile. "If not for them, I do not know what would have happened to any of us."

"You are right." She grinned when he pulled her on top of him so that she straddled his hips. His large cock swelled up against her belly and she took it in her hand, sliding her fingers up and down the solid length.

"Greedy man," she said, although she was just as greedy as he was. She loved her husband's body, knew that she could never get enough. She could only hope that they would forever be this happy and content.

Guiding her onto his length, he released a moan as he sank into her an inch at a time, until the head of his cock touched her womb.

Sunlight shone through the crack of the drapes, directly onto Shannon's beautiful body. He cupped her pert breasts, his thumbs brushing over the small, pink peaks of her nipples. "Your breasts seem bigger to me."

She smiled. "Aye, love, they usually grow when a woman becomes pregnant."

His eyes widened. "You are with child?"

"I believe so," she said, hoping he was as happy as she was.

Ever so slowly, a wide smile spread across his face and he kissed her. She started to ride him, and his fingers slid around her waist; she could see him looking for other signs of her pregnancy. She smiled, knowing he could look all he wanted, but she was only weeks along.

They came together and then he fell on the bed beside her,

enfolding her in his arms, their limbs wrapped around each other. "I can hardly wait to see our child."

"It will be a while yet, my love."

"My family will be ecstatic. Three grandchildren in quick succession. All our children will grow up together. Can you imagine if we all have girls?"

Or boys—would they have the same wicked reputations as their fathers?

She touched the scar on his shoulder that was still pink and puckered, and gently kissed it. "Do you realize this wound is responsible for us being together?"

"Are you saying you're happy I was shot?"

She laughed under her breath. "Of course not. I was worried sick about you."

"You were tough to seduce."

She lifted a brow. "You seduced me? I thought I was the one who seduced you."

He looked surprised at that, and she laughed under her breath. Months ago, when she had come to England, she had never imagined that she would marry a handsome young lord, or that the man would be one of the infamous Rakehells of Rochester. And yet against all odds, she had found the man of her dreams, married him, and now she carried his child.

He cupped her face with a large palm. "Before our child is born, I want to take you and Zach to Ireland."

She lifted her cheek from his chest. "Do you mean it?"

"Yes, once Zachary is fit to travel, of course."

"How long will we stay?"

"As long as you wish."

Her greatest desire was to take Zachary home, to help him rebuild his life, but most of all, to help them both bury the ghosts of their past and begin again.

And she was off to a wonderful start, with an impossibly beautiful man, who had made all her dreams come true.

Lord and Lady Rochester stood on the balcony of their bedchamber at Claymoore Hall and looked over the lush, green lawns where they had watched their sons grow from boys to men.

"Well, I can hardly believe we have finished what we set out to do mere months ago, Lord Rochester. Our boys are married and will soon be fathers."

Lord Rochester kissed the top of Betsy's head. "Indeed, you are a woman of your word. You always have been. You did well, my dear."

She smiled. "I did nothing. They undermined me at every turn and ignored my choices for them. But I admit when I am defeated. I was never very good at matchmaking."

"How right you are."

She looked up at him with furrowed brows. "You are not supposed to agree with me, my lord."

He chuckled. "Do you not remember when you tried to match me up with your cousin?"

"Yes, well . . . I had thought you liked her."

"I was only befriending her to get to you."

She smiled at the memory, remembering the exaltation she felt when he had started pursuing her in earnest. She had been the envy of every woman that season. Indeed, she could hardly believe the handsome earl had singled her out of all the young debutantes that summer.

"And what of the time you set up an encounter with your brother and your friend, Lady Dash?"

Recalling the horribly botched rendezvous, Betsy shrugged. "Stop now," she said crossly, but nestled against his chest, her heart lurching when she realized he had lost even more weight. She did not want to lose her lover, husband and friend.

"I remember when I brought you here to Claymoore Hall for our honeymoon. What a beautiful day."

"It was a beautiful day," she whispered, recalling the moment as though it had been just yesterday and not thirty-three years ago. Her heart had been pounding a million miles an hour as she stepped from the carriage and looked up at the servants who lined up on the staircase, ready to meet their new mistress.

She had felt so undeserving. Honestly, a part of her still did. She'd had such a wonderful life.

"I wouldn't change a thing, Betsy," he said, his voice thick with emotion. "Not a single moment."

She turned in his arms, looked up into his weathered face, and smiled. "Nor I."

She knew their days together were limited and was grateful for all that they had seen and experienced through the years. Theirs was a love built on a strong foundation, and God willing, their sons would experience a similar kind of love with their wives. The kind of love that came along just once in a lifetime.